BLUE WATERS

A TAINTED WATER NOVELLA

BOOK ONE OF TAINTED WATER SERIES

BY INDIA R ADAMS

First Edition: February 2016

Blue Waters is published by India's Productions

India R Adams
Empowering Perfect Imperfections

Editor: Karen Allen with Red Adept Editing and Lauren McKellar
Cover: Pro Book Covers
Formatting: Streetlight Graphics

Dedicated to the ones who have been waiting.

PREFACE

THERE WAS A BEAUTY IN dying that day, one I did not expect when I'd imagined meeting my maker. The blue water I sank through was angelic, quiet, peaceful. Link glided through the crystal waters as if he belonged to the gods of lakes and rivers. A lake was killing me that day. No, I take that back; my *decisions* were killing me that day, and he knew what decision had been made.

The sun shined, lighting the way as I sank farther and farther. His youthful-yet-wise eyes were so painfully determined to reach me, not to let me go, so determined to see my attempt fail.

My one hand graciously floated above me as my weighted foot led my final descent. I'll never forget the touch of his skin after his fingers stretched then touched the tips of mine—a sensation recognized only by one passing… saying goodbye, giving up, surrendering to the life he or she no longer wanted to live.

I found a beauty in dying that day.

CHAPTER ONE

Link and Whit

I DIDN'T MIND BEING A LOOSE cannon, a classic case of a rebel without a cause. I rather enjoyed my path to self-destruction. Why not? I was the opposite of depressing, and I wasn't harming anyone—just having fun as my pathetic clock of life ticked away. Okay, maybe that did sound a *little* morbid, and there was probably no maturity in such thoughts. But I felt if someone could've proved to me that there were *fun* in maturity, I would've shown you a sudden and magical transformation—if it were more fun than I was already having, that was.

The only person who had the ability to keep my 'live life to its fullest' mission at a moderate level was Link, a young soul cursed with an unending loyalty to me. Like me, he was one of the lucky ones. We had both managed to sustain our consciences and not let our money corrode our humanity. Our fat wallets—courtesy of our parents—never owned our free-spirited hearts, even though the money laced with lies ruled everything else, including love. We treated the less fortunate with the respect they deserved and secretly envied them because we knew firsthand money couldn't fill endless voids. In fact, it deepened voids and loneliness that one day, only he and I together would be able to heal...

As we sat in the dark, smelling the expensive leather of his overpriced car, his deep voice rumbled, "You ready?"

Is any teenager ready? No, but that was what made all this so invigorating.

"The question is," I playfully inquired, "are you?"

I understood that Link—formally known as Reether Jones—was the ultimate package, tall, strong, and handsome with dark hair. I should've felt more than fortunate to be sitting alone with him, but not one part of me wanted him in that manner. In a complicatedly way, Link was my very best friend. Oh yes, his girlfriend, Constance, *hated* me. She wasn't exactly on my favorite person list either.

Link chuckled mischievously. "Born, baby. Born ready."

And that was why I loved him. In my eyes, Link was a complete badass. He was witty, sharp-minded, and bighearted, and I had yet to meet anyone who compared. Not that I let Link and his well-nourished ego know this because, well, where was the fun in that? Someone had to keep the heartthrob grounded, so I happily nominated myself for the challenge.

"Please," I joked. "You were *born* so I could *beat* you—like every time."

Underneath all the ridiculous expectations placed on Link and myself was our bond. We were the same, born into stuck-up families we practically despised. Link was being groomed for Yale, for law, like his father, but all he wanted was to be a professional football player. His incredibly large and strong physique was made for such an aggressive sport, but his father felt it was beneath him.

I was to go to Harvard for the medical program even though the sight of blood made my knees weak, and the only thing my knees wanted to do was dance. Since I was not as easily refused, my parents compromised to keep me quiet for the time being and fed my hunger by letting me dance temporarily until it was time to 'grow up' and face the path carved out for me.

Creases formed around Link's inquisitive, electric blue eyes as he grinned. "Popcorn our wager?"

"Large!"

Link burst out laughing. "Not falling for that again!"

"*Small* popcorn." I grumbled to myself for being such a fool as I looked out his passenger window. In the corner of my eye, I saw Link's strong hand grip his door handle as he started our countdown. "One." I pulled my small mailbag over my head to secure it as my other hand eagerly gripped the passenger door handle. "Two." My adrenaline kicked in. "Three!" Link yelled, and we began our race.

Our doors swung open, and I leapt from the fancy car that labeled him, denying his true worth. No dollar amount could ever define Link's value. I slammed the door shut because that was one of our rules and took off for the front of the movie theater. Link's car beeped as he set his alarm.

I knew this win was mine as I heard his keys hit the ground, and he yelled, "Damn it!"

I howled in celebration as I ran as fast as I could across the theater's tiny parking lot. When my foot finally hit the long sidewalk, I heard our friend Harlan yell, "Whit, run!" I knew Link was coming up strong. I screamed, imagining his long legs gaining ground, and made my short legs go faster.

Even though Link adored me, he never let me win without earning it. I admired him for it because it always made me try harder and feel as if I had truly earned my success, something so simple—but so desired by both of us.

Harlan opened the front door, holding out my movie ticket. As I passed him in a blur, I grabbed my ticket and yelled, "Thank you." I skidded to a stop at the ticket collector's podium—the finish line. I high-fived his waiting hand as my nostrils detected delicious movie popcorn. Ford, whose incredible height always reminded me of my shortcomings, was collecting tickets. He smiled at my obvious win. "And he loses again!"

Out of breath, I said, "Getting off in time?"

Ford smirked. "Now don't *that* statement have a *double* meaning."

He leaned down so I could kiss his adorable cheek. I headed to the concession stand. "Perv. I'll save you a seat."

Coming through the door, Link bitched to whoever was willing to listen. "I dropped my keys. Otherwise, I totally had her."

"She cheats."

Aw, there's that horrid *voice.* Constance, Link's girlfriend, commented yet again on matters that did not concern her.

"When are you going to learn?" she continued. My shoulders tightened as her high heels clicked across the old flooring.

I refused to believe that Constance's beauty—overshadowing my own disastrous excuse for femininity—was the real fuel for our feuds.

To the oldest movie theater employee in the history of earth, who was waiting for my order, I said, "Yes, I will have a"—I stopped to grin over my shoulder to the jealous loser Link—"a *large* popcorn, please."

Frank chuckled as he typed on his register. "Not falling for that again?"

The elderly man clearly remembered the fit I threw at that very counter when I'd learned my best friend had cheated me out of my favorite snack.

That day, I'd gotten my prize, but it was only a *small.* Tricky Link always kept me on my toes.

"Nope. And don't hold back on the butter."

"All that butter is going to make her ass fat," mumbled Constance, as the rest of my friends caught up.

"Don't start, babe," Link warned his personal freak show.

I ignored Constance. "Frank, on *that* note, I'll take a Coke too—on Link's tab of course." I faced Constance and condescendingly asked, "Anything else?"

"You're a bitch?"

Instead of returning the hatred, I turned back to Frank. "And M&Ms, please."

"Hey!" Link laughed. "Why do *I* have to pay for *her* loud mouth?"

After Frank handed over the goods, I popped some of my crunchy, buttery, well-earned prize in my mouth. "Because Constance is a *constant* pain in my—"

"Okay." Harlan put his arm around my shoulders to wisely guide me away before I got to express the rest of my 'constant' thoughts.

"Let's go find some seats." Harlan stole a handful of popcorn, clearly still trying to distract me. I hollered my disapproval as he called over his shoulder to Link, "You'll get her M&M's and Coke?"

Link mumbled as he dug into his wallet. "You mean *my* Coke?"

"Why did you bring her?" I asked Harlan, as I was escorted down the hall toward our theater—one of the two in the rickety building.

Harlan lived near Constance, on the other side of the rural town in Connecticut where we attended school. Link and I lived on the opposite end. Link was supposed to be a pupil at the private school closer to our home, but he chose to follow me instead. The school with the dance program had the required elite status, so his parents allowed it. We'd planned our freshman year to be just the two of us against the world, but surrounded by unknowns in an unfamiliar school, we met Harlan and Ford. The four of us had caused chaos ever since.

Harlan looked down at me—as did most of the population. "Because your best friend thinks he's in love with her."

I ate more popcorn. "Ugh, don't remind me. I still can't comprehend this fact. Denial seems to be my best option at this point."

Harlan muttered, "I swear you and Reeth will marry someday."

I stopped walking, so I could deliver an adequate stink-eye. Harlan laughed. "Okay! So you have *two* issues you are in denial about. Got it." Harlan opened the theater door for me. "Whitney, if you'd give Connie a chance, you'd see she's actually pretty cool... when not hating on you, of course."

Harlan admitting to Connie being a bitch made me abandon my dirty look and move onward. As I sat in a theater seat with Harlan to my right, I thought about how I couldn't imagine being friends with the wench from hell, but I hated the thought of punishing Link for my personal tastes. It wasn't his fault that the girl had incredible endurance and chased him until he caved our senior year.

Just then, Link entered the theater and attempted to sit in the seat to the left of mine. Even though I was on the fence about forgiving him for falling for an alien in high heels, I complained. "Hey, I saved that seat for Ford."

"I can only handle one bitching out at a time, Whit." Link claimed the saved seat, his big shoulders promptly demanding some of my designated space, and seemed to have no regrets about his criticizing comment.

One should be offended, but Link was only checking me—keeping me in line, as I always did him.

Constance sat next to him. "I'm not a bitch."

"Here we go again." Link sighed, as if tired of being completely misunderstood.

Watching his jaded expression age him, I realized Constance and I were being selfish. A decent character like Link did not deserve to be tortured because he loved two girls. Or at least I believed he didn't. I knew his love for me was different, but it didn't stifle the way he felt for Connie. I found myself whispering "I'm sorry," thinking again about what Harlan had said as I leaned my head on his arm. I knew I needed to accept that my friend had feelings for someone.

In complete shock, Link looked at Harlan. "What did you say to her?"

"The truth." Harlan dared to stick his fingers in my bucket of popcorn again. He quickly retreated with a chuckle when I growled my final warning.

Ford walked in, and after one second of observation, he complained. "Whitney! My seat?"

I sat up and opened my mouth, but before I got to reply, Link answered for me. “Pick an outer seat, chump. I sit by my girls.”

Ford gestured to Harlan, who said, “Not moving. You win the prize.”

Ford eyed the winnings. “Connie? You settled yet?”

Apparently, he was also over our bitching.

The blond disaster answered, “What choice do I have? My boyfriend just called me a bitch.”

I felt compelled to help my partner in crime. I leaned forward. “Link meant that is how you are *acting*, and he… didn’t single you out… and, and, I… *possibly*… am to blame… for your… behavior.”

Okay, so some jaws hit the ground, but I was completely capable of swallowing a little pride for the most important person in my life. Link looking at me with a grin told me how much he loved me and how much he admired me. While Link kissed my forehead, I asked in shame, “Why do you put up with me?”

“Because under your fake tough exterior, there is a heart of gold. And because you are the cutest redhead in the world.” He whispered, “I love you, girl,” and handed me *my* Coke.

Feeling worthy again, I took a big swig and let my junk-fest begin.

As we settled properly into the seats that would own our asses for the next two hours, more patrons entered while Constance griped yet a-freaking-gain. “Why did we have to choose a dancing movie? Who cares about a ballerina’s struggles and boring drama?”

See? Constant pain in my—

“Babe! Enough!” Link snapped. “Whit just apologized to you. Do you have *any* clue what a rare event you just experienced?”

Ford whispered to her, “FYI? Never been done.”

“When pigs fly, I will accept *that* as an apology,” said the one the circus was hanging missing posters for. Constance and I were a work in progress.

“It’s the closest to one you may ever receive,” Link explained. “Please! Meet Whit halfway here, Connie. Damn.”

Harlan and Ford glared, informing Constance that they were one hundred percent behind Link. I knew this glare. I had been the recipient once—or many times.

Looking as if she felt the pressure of our clan’s judgment, Constance finally said, “Fine. I’m sure… this will be a good movie.” She leaned forward and looked over to me. "Thank you for the apology, and good choice of movie, Whitney."

Ford and Harlan looked around. Link's shoulders relaxed, and he chuckled at his next two challenges. "What are you two idiots doing?"

Still in search of something, Harlan and Ford spoke in unison. "Looking for the flying pigs."

As the theater darkened slightly, Link leaned to me. "Are you nervous?" He knew me, which meant he knew what was truly on my mind—not the movie. I'd just learned that day that I'd earned a dance audition I desperately wanted, and to fail meant my parents were right. "Nah, I got some congratulations and some expected cold shoulders, but I'm good."

Link's eyes studied me. "Whit." He clearly saw through my lie.

I looked directly into his big ol' blues and aggressively nodded. I was. I was so nervous about my upcoming audition that I could've puked, but I didn't want to waste any of the delicious popcorn that I was noticing to be a little dry.

"Where are you going now?" Link asked, as I stood up.

"Frank shorted me on my butter. Old bastard knows better." I accidently stepped on Link's big foot, causing him to yelp in pain.

"Aren't dancers supposed to be graceful or something?" Ford teased me as I tripped past him.

Harlan clarified an apparent fact. "Whit's a graceful klutz at best."

As I ran out the door, tripping once again—on my own two feet this time—I loudly whispered, "Ford, have them hold the movie 'til I get back." As an employee of the establishment, I felt he should have some pull.

"I'm a ticket boy, not God."

I ran to the concession counter to see Frank had abandoned his post. Without an employee in sight, and a movie guy refusing to push pause, I took my only option. I climbed over the counter to get my own damn butter.

As I was falling off the other side of the counter—after a shameful ass-in-the-air presentation—it was evidently clear Harlan was right. I might have been one hell of a dancer, and had a rare audition with Tender West's summer dance program, but I truly was a complete klutz.

After pulling myself off a filthy floor, I wiped questionable grease off my palms and mailbag and grabbed my bucket of popcorn—and yes, I refilled it, deciding I was a regular and deserved a couple of free kernels.

Feeling giddy at finally having control over the infamous butter machine, I swore angels sung in harmony, and I smiled and squealed in delight.

When I heard a chuckle behind me, my nervous stealing hands threw my bucket of popcorn up into the air, announcing my guilt. I turned to see who had busted me and looked into the most mysterious, trouble-promising, male blue eyes in the whole wide world.

CHAPTER TWO

Franky and Crash

THE ROUGH-LOOKING CHARACTER WITH DARKER hair and a medium-sized scar above his left eyebrow stood on the 'proper' side of the counter, where I should have been, and watched popcorn fall from my unruly red hair. "Damn, sorry to have scared you. I just need a water. How much will it be?"

Fighting the desire to lick the individual before me, I uttered, "Uh," before looking up at the price menu on the wall behind me. "Ummm a dollar seventy-five… Damn! They charge a buck seventy-five for a water? That is redunkulous!"

As tatted fingers reached into a leather wallet, Mr. Lickable said, "You have unusual sale tactics."

Being a tad bit stunned by this guy, who pleasantly appeared to be everything mamas warn young girls about, I was slow to realize he thought I was a theater employee. Since *my* mother never took the time to warn me about such things, and turning down an opportunity for a good time was against my religion, I agreed. "That's what the owner said in my job interview. Yep! That's me: Franket."

Tilting his head and exposing a partially tattooed neck, he asked, "Your name is Franket?" The tattoo saying, "Life 1982" was clearly significant, but it being along his jugular seemed even more so.

I shrugged. "I know. My parents must hate me, right?"

He grinned, and I was instantly intrigued, especially when the stranger said, "Far too cute to be a Franket, but I think you can *more* than pull off a Franky. Do you mind?"

This stranger danger could've decided to rename me 'Mug Rat El

Stinky,' and I would've still replied, "Works for me! My mom may not like it, but she needs to pipe it down anyway, or I'm telling my dad she's sleeping with the pool boy."

"You have a pool boy, yet you work here?"

"Not *my* pool boy, remember? Mother's pool toy—I mean boy."

"You're a natural born hell-raiser, ain't cha?"

I approved of his approving tone. Then I thought of what my Link had said earlier. "Born ready." I reached into the fridge for the water bottle and set it on the counter. "That'll be one seventy-five."

"No tax?"

"Huh?"

Mr. Lickable snickered. "There's more of that talent you must've been hired for."

"Like you said, Mr. Water Purchaser, I'm cute. Probably how I got the job, right?"

"I'd hire you." Somehow, I understood he was implying more, but I played along.

"You have a movie theater?"

"Nope."

"Sorry. Seems you and I are over before we ever even began."

"Oh, something has begun here, and you and I both know it."

Boy, did I! I gripped the counter so I wouldn't humiliate myself by throwing my willing body right back over the counter where I had come from, offering myself on a popcorn platter. Ah, but playing hard to get was so much more fun, so I had to do it. "Sorry, on the clock. And I have three mouths to feed, so I've gotta keep earning my pathetic excuse for a paycheck."

He playfully shook his head. "How old are you? Mouths to feed?"

"Yeppers. My adopted boys. Reether, Harlan, and Ford. And I'm seventeen. Jailbait for you, I presume?"

"I'd take my chances with jail time, but I'm not ready for kids, Franky."

"Too late. I'm a package deal."

He put down a five on the counter. "Damn. Well, at least keep the change—for your boys."

"Had every intention to." I watched the bad boy in the making slip from my incapable grasp. His black T-shirt was snug, taunting me to take a gander at shoulders that were surely strong and perfectly molded, but I got preoccupied with his snug jeans that ever-so-gently caressed the cutest ass known to man. I whispered to myself, "Here's to one-sided mental affairs."

I gasped when I saw another tattoo on the back of his neck, along his spinal cord. It read, "Death 1995." We were in 2013.

Back in my fake movie employee position, I aggressively pushed buttons, trying to open the register. The damn machine screamed and beeped at me until Frank finally returned to his post and asked with an amused tone, "What are you doing?"

"Trying to rob the joint. What does it look like?"

"Like you're trying to rob the joint." Frank ran his hand through his silver hair as if lost for other words.

The drawer popped open, and I cheered and took out three bucks. I handed Frank Mr. Lickable's five while slipping the change— my hard-earned dough—in my pocket. As he stared at the cash in his hand, I explained. "For the water I just sold. Oh, by the way, I need a new popcorn." I pointed to my popcorn—now all over, well, everything.

Frank held out his other palm.

"Damn it." I handed over my three bucks for the new bucket of kernels. "Don't. Forget. Extra. Butter! Look what you *not* doing so has caused me. I have questionable goo on my hands, I had to lie to a hot guy, and now, I'm without the three bucks in my pocket that I dishonestly earned. Oh, and my name is Franky if some luscious blue-eyed creature happens to inquire about your redheaded employee."

"What?"

By the time I was heading back into the theater, the movie had started, and Ford had fallen asleep, as usual. It was a good thing he always got in for free. Since Ford was in Snoozeville, he was unable to retract his size fourteens and caused another Whit fall down. After flying past Connie—who did nothing to help—my popcorn once again escaped my hands. Staring at the ground because I was shamefully on my hands and knees, I whispered to Link, "Did you save my popped kernels? Please tell me you did."

With my precious bucket of popcorn in his talented, football-catching hands, Link whispered, "Yes. Now get in your seat before that ballerina jumps off the big screen and beats you for such a poor representation of the dancer race."

He yelped again as I once more stepped on his foot. I whispered, "Oops, sorry!" sat down, and reached into my mailbag.

"Skittles?"

"Frank couldn't resist my charm."

"What about your M&M's in my pocket?"

"Hand them over."

Harlan—the smart-ass, leaned in. "Your ass is going to burst out of your tutu."

"I'm a modern dancer. No tutus required, numb nuts."

When the movie ended, I received dirty looks from my friends. "How was I to know she was going to go all ballerina mental and kill herself at the end?"

I teased, but really, I was profoundly affected by the serenity of her passion, her commitment to sacrifice everything for love. The pointe shoe was just a symbol—a metaphor for her desire—being ripped from her. I had experienced loss, incredible loss, but never passion that would've made me to not want to live.

Link laughed. "Whit! She did *not* kill herself! She dove into the water to get that hard-toed, pink dance-shoe thingy, and, well those strappy things got stuck on the log, and-and she… self-sacrificed for her love of dancing."

Harlan stretched across me and cupped Link's testicles. Link swatted him away. "What are you doing?"

"Seeing if they're still there."

Ford blinked awake. "Why is Harlan molesting Link's balls?"

Connie whined, "Because he's all emotional over the dumb ballerina killing herself."

Ford stretched and yawned, trying to wake up. "Killing her—what the hell did I miss?"

As everyone stood, I climbed up onto my seat. "But seriously, dancer to dancer, I'm emotionally scarred and vulnerable, and I'm now in need of a ride."

Link put his back to me so I could climb aboard. "Emotionally scarred, my ass. You're just lazy." As my legs wrapped his waist, more Link comments commenced. "Jesus, Whit, you already weigh more 'cause of the gallon of popcorn, two bags of candy, and *my* large Coke."

Exiting the theater on my personal chariot, I threw away my trash over Link's shoulder. Of course, he complained. "I think you got butter on my shirt."

My arms attempted to choke Link until I heard, "Franky?"

With one eye closed and wondering how to explain my next lie, I looked at Mr. Lickable, and wouldn't you know it, he looked even hotter. The hallway was full of people exiting the other movie theater, and he had four equally scary-looking thugs flanking him. They were older, dressed a little more professionally, but each had the same presence, the kind that silently warned you to watch your step. Mr. Lickable smirked at me riding piggyback on Link. "Another questionable employee tactic?"

"Yes, as a matter a fact, it is. I am a highly trained, uh, ticket stub collector and this"—I pointed to my ride—"sly non-ticket stub holder thought he could escape my ticket stub radar."

"What?" Link tried to eyeball me over his shoulder while I expertly maneuvered to avoid his scrutiny.

Getting back to Mr. Lickable, I said, "As you can see… he failed… and I am currently in the process of subduing him 'til… the, uh, ticket stub police come to complete this arrest."

Constance rolled her eyes, pecked Link's lips, and sneered in my general direction. "I'm going to the ladies' room. I'm suddenly feeling nauseous."

The kiss seemed to clarify whether or not Link and I were an item because Mr. Lickable nodded to his posse. "Meet ya outside." The four mysterious silent ones walked away as he eagerly held up his ticket stub for me to see. "Clearly, I have not committed the same offense. Am I clear to proceed?" His smile dared me to keep up our entertaining charade.

With the challenge accepted, I slid off my best friend's back. Link intently observed me with the new guy, and his expression showed me he was questioning the banter. I told my new interest, "Unfortunately, my ticket stub senses—due to my extensive training—"

Mr. Lickable nodded, playing along. "Yes, top secret ticket stub training."

"Exactly! My senses tell me that I must see your ID to make sure you are not a… uh, prior offender."

"Whit, what are you up to now?" An accusing look appeared in Link's eyes.

"Whit? Not Franky?" Mr. Lickable asked.

Link reached over me, offering his palm for a handshake. "Since 'Franky' here is rude, I'll introduce myself. Reether Jones."

"Nice to meet you, Reether. Wait…" Mr. Lickable paused possibly thinking about Link's true name. In the background, I heard Harlan and Ford cooing horrid pick-up lines to some girls walking by. "*Hey* there, beautiful… How *you* doing?…"

My witty stranger said, "Let me guess. Ford and Harlan?"

Hearing their names, my two other, supposedly adopted sons turned to us. "What up?"

Mr. Lickable grinned. "Did my change help feed your sons dinner?"

Link, Harlan, and Ford all looked at one another. I answered their silent question. "No, but it did buy them popcorn."

"Hey!" Harlan complained. "You growled at me when I tried to have some of that—"

"Shush," I scolded my overgrown child. "Don't sass your mother."

Link's hands rested on my shoulders. "And apparently, you have already met our imaginative mother, Whitney."

Under my breath, I explained, "Whitney is my undercover name, but you and I are already past that."

"Okay, Franky it is." The young man handed me an ID.

"*Harold* Thompson?" I practically shouted. "I see your parents hate you too?"

Harold took back his ID, grinning. "More than you know." He opened his hand to expose his waiting palm. "Only fair."

I slowly reached into my small mailbag for my ID. "I don't play fair, Harold. That's something you should know up front—oh, and we gotta work on that name of yours, by the way, and find you a suitable nickname, like my Link."

I went to hand my ID over, but Link snatched it from my hand. "Sorry, *Mom* here seems to have her idiot cap on, thinking she's just going to hand over her personal information to a complete stranger."

Over my shoulder, I looked up at Link. "But have you seen his blue eyes?" Looking into Link's blue eyes had my attraction wandering.

"Link?" Mr. Lickable asked.

Refocused, I stepped aside to be able to see both guys and patted Link's chest. "Yep! Every chain is only as strong as its weakest link. And since this poor sucker—my best friend—is crazy for me and spoils the shit out of me, he's my weakest link. I love our dysfunctional ways."

Harold smiled, and my heart was stolen. "By the looks of it, he seems to be your strongest link, Franky."

My heart skipped a beat. I had been told this before.

"And," Harold added, "actually, I already have a nickname—that is, if you approve of it, of course."

This Harold was proving to be highly intelligent. I gestured for him to proceed. "To be determined. Let's hear it."

"Crash."

As my internal gorgeousness radar went into overdrive, I fell into Link and grabbed his shirt. "Did Harold just get even hotter to you?"

"Uh, didn't find Harold hot to begin with." Link glanced up. "No offense, dude."

Harold—Crash—raised his hands. "None taken, I suppose. I *was* going to ask for your number, but now I see that the attraction is clearly one-sided."

My forehead fell to Link's chest. "And he's funny, Link! I must marry him."

"Welcome to the family, pops," Ford chimed in.

After getting my excitement under control, I inhaled deeply, turned around, and announced to Crash, "It has been decided. This Friday night, after I go roller skating with these peeps"—I thumb-gestured behind me—"I will be starving, so *you* may take me out to dinner. That gives you a few days to recover from your emotional—and possibly one-sided—sexual connection with Link."

Crash bowed his head. "Thank you for your consideration and time to heal."

Just then, Connie walked up. "He sure sounds more educated than he looks."

"Okay," said Harlan, as he did his second distraction for the night, leading Connie away.

An extremely awkward moment presented itself. Constance had just showed the ugly side of money, but Crash just smirked. "Link? Is that the reason for my denial?"

I busted out laughing so hard surrounding patrons jumped. "Okay, you just earned an invitation to skating—I might even pay your way." I leaned to him and whispered so all could hear. "But I don't really claim *her*. Just my guys."

Crash looked at Link with sympathy. "That must make your life quite interesting."

Ford rolled his eyes. "You have no idea. Poor sucker."

Crash looked back at me. "Aren't we a little old for roller skating?"

I closed my eyes in annoyance. "Crash, do *not* ruin this perfect union by insulting eighties night."

"But you weren't even born yet."

My eyes opened. "In spirit, I was already here—with big hair, may I add. Besides, you have to see Ford on wheels singing 'Like a Virgin' by Madonna."

Crash grabbed his stomach laughing, clearly already visualizing what could only be described as a riot. Ford was 6'3" and no more than a buck forty soaking wet.

Ford said, "I might body roll around on the ground for this special occasion—finding a new daddy and all."

Feeling that I had to always exit with the upper hand, I started walking away. I had Crash right where I wanted him. "See ya, Friday, Crash." There was only one skating rink in our two local towns and one big city, so I knew he'd find his way. To my guys, I said, "Sons, let's travel." They said their goodbyes and followed.

Behind me, Crash said, "Hey, how do you know I don't have a girlfriend or something and won't be there Friday night?"

I never turned around, just hollered, "'Cause your eyes are all over my ass."

Link's big feet stumbled over each other. "Whit!"

"Well, is he?"

Ford looked back. "That's an affirmative, *Mom*."

The security guard waved Link's car through our neighborhood gate. "Good evening, Miss Summers, Mr. Jones."

We waved. "Hey, John."

"Miss Summers, Miss Maria recently left for the day."

My mother somehow did not see the stereotype when hiring an illegal

Mexican immigrant to scrub her imported toilets. Maria was sweet and usually gone before I got home from school, so I wondered what extra chore my mom had put on her list to keep Maria from her family so late.

I lived across the lake from Link. The rear of our homes—that screamed, "status"—faced each other, giving Link and me easy access to one another. I could always look out my bedroom window and see Link's bedroom light. It calmed me just seeing the glow, knowing he was in there, reading or resting, and not too far from me. Every night, he blinked his light to tell me good night.

My three-story house was lit up when we arrived. My parents' security system turned on lights automatically when they were out of town—which unfortunately was more often than not—so that I would not come home to a dark house.

"Love ya, girl."

I kissed Link's cheek and got out of his car. "Thanks for a hell of a night."

After walking inside, I reset the alarm and went into the kitchen for a glass of milk. As the cool beverage slid down my throat, I looked around my home. Thousands and thousands of dollars worth of furniture and items surrounded me. I wish I could brag about the grand colors that my mother favored, how her style and décor represented and expressed her love for life, but I can't because she always picked safe bland colors to not stick out and open herself to judgment. She was all too familiar with judgment, being an unfair judge and jury all on her own.

In fact, the priceless, useless decorations offered emptiness and were downright absurd. My mother insisting on buying items she never stayed home to enjoy reminded me of her shallow ways. I guess owning them was enough for her to feel fulfilled, or somehow significant, in a materialistic, competitive world.

Not able to stomach the proof of her ridiculous inadequacy for another moment, I walked straight up the stairs to finish my milk. There was no one to talk to, so there was no reason to look for anyone, but I did.

At his bedroom door, I knocked our three-knock rhythm. When there was no answer, I went to my room, wondering if I was crazy for trying.

CHAPTER THREE

Swimmers and Stalkers

My phone ringing woke me. It was always wonderful to awake to a cold, unwanted conversation first thing in the morning. "Hello?"

"How was your movie, dear?"

I'd already known who it was before she spoke—the same woman who decorated my bedroom in gray, white and black. My room looked and felt like a morgue cleaned with bleach: morbid colors representing the lack of life—just like the woman on the other end of the phone. "Good morning, Mother. The movie was very informative. How is Father's convention?"

"Splendid, dear. Wish you could be with us, but, well, it looks better to the public eye to keep you in school. You understand, yes?"

"Of course, Mother," I replied, faintly mocking her because I didn't. I couldn't comprehend why she would rather be on the road than with her own child, but who was I to stop our routine of deceit and speak the truth out loud? "Is Father available?"

"No, dear. You know he's busy."

"Yes, I do," I said, wishing otherwise.

When I was a little girl, I could make him smile once in a while. It wasn't much but better than my mother's reactions. My very presence seemed to annoy her as if I was a child misplaced into her care, who she wished would disappear. Since I was unable to quench her unspoken desire, she stuck me in frilly hats, tucked away my hair—seemingly hoping to camouflage me while in the presence of the upper class—and told me to be quiet wherever we went. To her disappointment, I grew up to be the opposite, an expressive conversationalist with my red curls flying in the wind.

"Well, I'm off for my morning swim. Please send Father my love."

"Delightful, dear. Tell Reether hello. I will call tomorrow morning, as usual."

I walked out my back French doors, and the peaceful misty morning air greeted me. My only nearby neighbors—who lived a football field away—were still sleeping. It was still so early. I saw Link already waiting on his back patio. He was too far away for me to be sure, but I sensed him smiling his dare from across the lake. Grinning, I exaggeratedly laid down my towel, accepting his challenge. He witnessed the green light and responded, setting down his own plush towel. I took off my robe, starting our countdown. We both took off running.

We crossed our huge big backyards—meant to entertain our parents' shallow acquaintances—with a vengeance and sprinted, laughing, down our boat docks. Arms took positions over our heads as our feet pushed us off the end of our wooden planks. I took a deep breath every time I dove into that blue water for two reasons.

One: So that I had the oxygen needed.

Two: Because I hoped for the feeling I once had…

All my private lessons came to the forefront of my mind, and I raced to the middle of the lake, hoping to be able to scream, "I won," but when Link did not resurface, I cussed, knowing he was staying underwater. That was where Link preferred to be. He once told me it was because of the sounds and because he felt at peace there. Underwater was also where Link exceled with his speed, and apparently his ego was still bruised from me winning the race last night. Link was out for revenge, and I was going to lose.

I pumped my arms and legs faster to no avail. Link popped to the surface, arriving to the center before me with a satisfied expression. Water dripped from his conniving grin. He asked, "Oatmeal?" as if I had a choice.

I treaded water. "*I* win and get buttery popcorn. *You* win, and I'm forced to eat *oatmeal*."

"One: It's healthy. Two: Everything needs balance, baby."

We swam back to his house where his parents' maid welcomed us with two warmed bathrobes and two steaming bowls on their back patio. She smiled. "Good morning, Miss Whitney. Mr. Reether insisted today would be his win. Don't worry. I put extra butter and honey in the oats for you."

After wrapping myself in the toasty robe, I sat on the outside furniture that most people would feel blessed to have *inside* their homes. "Thank you. I appreciate your pity because Mr. Link sucks."

I had a dance rehearsal after school, so I opted to drive myself instead of carpooling with Link to save gas. Entering the parking lot, I slowly swerved around students, all dressed in the same blue and green uniform as mine, standing in the middle of the lane, completely oblivious to oncoming traffic. Speakers thumped favorite songs, and voices carried the latest gossip.

The school building used to be a convent that had been shut down for over fifty years, so it had a cool authentic aged look. It was secluded because it had been a nunnery, so we got to attend school with some nature around us. Tall trees reaching for the sky helped balance out the fake folks inside the damned building.

Pulling into my sometimes-regular parking spot put me right next to Link's car. That put me right next to tongues swapping between Connie and Link and had me wanting to ralf my oatmeal all over Link's freshly waxed car. Connie moaned, making me roll my eyes and internally gag as I got out of my own vehicle—a Mercedes that my mom insisted I drive—so I treated it as my personal dumpster. I got a warning look from Harlan, who was a row over, waiting for me next to his truck, a spectacular 1950 black Ford truck that was the symbol of his permanent middle finger to the snob society of our school. Rebellion at its finest.

"Really?" I walked toward him, thumbing over my shoulder. "It does nothing violent to your stomach?"

Leaving the acquaintances he'd been talking to, Ford ran up next to me. "Oh, we must be talking about the sucking fishes behind us."

I heard Sue, a dancer girlfriend of mine, scream as she ran toward me. She grabbed my hands and whispered, "We made it."

Ford and Harlan cheered for us. Link had kept his promise and told no one what my teacher had confided in me.

My school was mostly a normal private school with the addition of an arts program. It had top-notch facilities for the elite wannabe artists with no clue how to break a sweat. The scholarship students with no means except their talent—including Cindy, smiling and waiting for my response—had my utmost respect.

Tender West, the modern dance company, had only offered auditions to three dancers, and I was one of them. Constance wasn't the only one who hated me. Now there were the remaining rich, uninvited dancers waiting to trip me, hoping for an "accidental" injury to make room for them.

The fact that the two scholarship students were among the invited didn't shock me. Modern dance and most choreography in general come from the heart—something that affects us deeply, such as experiences of loss and sorrow. The two scholarship students came from what was considered to be the projects, so other students looked down on them, but in truth, those hardships gave them raw emotions to pull from. The two girls embodied soul-driven desire, a prime example of why one should never judge based in income.

My dance teacher's name was Mrs. Pomerantzeff—Mrs. P. for short. Mrs. P. was also a redhead but, unlike myself, she was quiet, soft. She led her pupils—in and out of the dance studio—with class and love. Mrs. P. had already told me I was chosen for an audition and that Tender West was coming to see us, but truth be told, I had a very small chance of being accepted. Again, I felt the anxiety and pressure of such an honor.

"You deserve this," I told Cindy. "You worked your ass off." I hugged her, but there was only one person who could settle my building nerves. I released Cindy and turned to find him, hoping to not be forced to witness more slobber exchanging. He was done kissing Constance. In fact, she was nowhere to be found. Link smiled at me with such adoration that I knew he understood.

I mouthed, *I can do this?*

Link nodded. "Better than anyone I know."

If Link believed I could, I knew it was possible. I inhaled, mouthed, *okay*, and mentally prepared myself for the soon-to-come biggest moment of my young dancer career.

I had four advanced academic classes before lunch then three hours of dance classes every afternoon. During my first period, my phone vibrated in my pocket. I secretively pulled it out but didn't recognize the number. I read the message:

I don't know how to skate

I gasped in sudden glee to see words from Mr. Lickable, then wrote:

How'd u get my digits?

Crash's words appeared:

As Link's mean girl said, I'm not as dumb as I look

I was too shocked and excited to write back and explain that he was the opposite of dumb-looking in my eyes. Soon, my phone vibrated again:

That ok?

Pulling my giddy self back together, I wrote:

Depends. U a stalker?

Yep! Cool with that?

Hmmm. Where we going for din-din?

LOL Chuck E Cheese 50 free tokens

In that case u can stalk all u want

Have a great day, Franky

I thought about how my ass must have looked better in those jeans than I'd thought and that Friday night couldn't come fast enough.

The dance classroom was one of my favorite rooms in the old building. It had beautiful, paned windows—like the windows in the church that had been converted into a theater. Sunbeams would shine through, showing the magnificent colors. The dance room had new sprung wood floors, but on a warm day I could almost smell the history of the abandoned convent. I was thinking of the nuns when I heard Mrs. P.'s gentle voice, "Whitney, Cindy, and Alexis, next week I need to know what audition songs you have chosen." We all stood in leotards and footless tights as our teacher explained which dancer was pairing up with which instructor and how my rigorous rehearsal schedule was about to intensify because we were already working on our senior projects. Three hours later, I was saying goodbye to my fellow dancers, who were leaving for the day. I was to stay behind to show Mrs. P. another part of the routine I'd choreographed for my senior project.

Two hours later, I dragged my exhausted ass across the school parking lot to climb into my junk-infested car, go home, and pass out without even taking a much-needed shower, but I saw a delightfully sinister character, dressed partially in leather, wearing ripped jeans, leaning against my car.

"Thought I was joking about stalking you?" Crash asked.

I didn't know where it came from, but I was suddenly reenergized. "I was hoping not."

Mr. Lickable eyed me from head to toe. "So, a dancer, huh?"

"Somebody has to do it, right?"

Crash grinned. "Yeah, I guess so."

I noticed a bruise on his cheek and teased, "Piss someone off?" I pointed to his face. "Trying to match that scar above your eyebrow?"

He touched the spot on his cheek as if he had forgotten about it. "Oh, yeah. I mean, no." When he touched his old scar, he squinted. "Uh, just felt like running my face into a wall. Again. Hungry?"

I nodded in thought about his poor excuse but only said, "I'm not in shape for public." I pointed down to my sticky self.

As if he found me delicious, Crash said, "Not sure I want to share you with the public."

"Sweaty sweatpants are your weakness?"

"They are now." Crash looked me over again—which I thoroughly enjoyed. "Want a pizza? Takeout of course. We can eat at my place."

"Want Link up your ass?"

He stood up straight, as if he'd crossed an unwanted barrier. "I thought you two weren't an item."

"Relax, we're not, but he's not kidding about being protective. I go to your house, where you can possibly take advantage of me because of a carb overdose, and things might end badly for you."

He relaxed again. "Your house then?"

I grimaced. "Not sure if that's any better. My parents are out of town."

"What if I promise not to take advantage of you in a pepperoni-induced coma?"

"Deal."

"Can I have a lift?"

"No ride?"

Crash looked over to a black car with dark-tinted windows parked by the quiet road, leading to the now deserted school parking lot. The mysterious car didn't scream, "driven by a young adult," but I said, "Oh, you can follow me then."

He nodded to the car. It drove away. "I'll just ride with you."

Since I was quite confident the car didn't drive away on its own, I thought about the large men flanking him the night we'd met. "Same friends from the movie?"

"Something like that."

"What's with your security detail?"

"Nothing worth mentioning."

I should've asked for more specifics, but I figured to do so would've left me having to answer any questions Crash had about my parents. With such a pleasant distraction in the form of a handsome young man, well, I just didn't want to dredge up unpleasant history.

"So, for now we leave family drama out of getting to know each other?"

Crash raised a fist for me to bump. "Franky's the bomb." He let out a breath I hadn't known he was holding.

I was sure my housekeeper had my fridge fully stocked with healthy crap, but I didn't have the self-control to turn down some Italian pie. After picking up pizzas, I checked in my rearview mirror and giggled. "Your friends have returned." I glanced over at Crash and realized he was staring in the passenger side mirror of my car.

"Was hoping you wouldn't notice."

At my security gate, I pointed behind me. "Plus one tonight."

John looked at the car behind mine then quietly asked, "Everything okay, Miss Whitney?"

I smiled but wasn't sure of the answer. "Yep, I'm good."

Crash didn't seem impressed in the slightest with my expensive neighborhood as we drove through it, and that was kind of nice. I had *friends* who liked to come over for the experience of living large. Maybe I was spoiled or simply ungrateful, but I felt I didn't *belong* and that all my parent's money had come with a heavy cost. And it had. Possibly, it always does.

Walking out my back door with two pizza boxes in hand, Crash took a gander. "Umm, so how is it exactly that your mom is having an affair with a pool boy when you are lacking the main ingredient?"

Busted! "Are you questioning my mom's affair, simply because of the fact that I have no pool? Crash, I thought you were more inventive than that."

He laughed, rolling his eyes. "What was I thinking, adding one plus one and coming up with two?"

I led him to the dock. "It's okay. I forgive you."

Sitting at the edge of my dock with open pizza boxes, Crash asked, "Trying to romance me with the sun setting and the beautiful blue water?"

I wished the dock was lower so our bare feet could touch the blue water Crash referred to. "Nah, not the romance kind of gal, Crash."

With his pizza almost to his mouth, Mr. Lickable sexily asked, "So what kind of girl are you?"

In spite of all my proper etiquette classes, I answered with a full mouth. "The mysterious, wonder-of-the-world kind."

Choking on his food, Crash laughed. "Confident much?"

Suddenly not in the mood to lie or kid around, I answered, "No… just a runner." Crash looked at me as if I had spoken words extremely familiar to him. "What?"

He shook his head. "I thought we were leaving family drama out of tonight."

I took another bite, wondering what Crash was running from.

"I like you, Franky," he said with unexpected sincerity.

I took a deep breath. We liked each other more quickly than was probably healthy, and my deep inhale seemed to be my body preparing for whatever that meant and what was to come. Before I could tell him I felt the same, "What the hell is going on?" echoed from across the lake. I proudly smiled with pizza in my teeth and yelled to Link, "Having sex!"

Fully clothed, Link dove into the water and swam toward me to beat my ass. Crash looked at me as if I'd just surrendered him to the enemy. I took a sip of my Coke. "No worries. He's coming for me—or for the pizza. It has yet to be determined."

"Uh… and if he's coming for me?"

"You might want to speed dial your security peeps."

Watching Link swim like a pro, Crash asked, "You swim a lot here?"

"I call it swimming. My brother called it sinking."

"Sinking?"

I wiped my mouth with a napkin. "He said my ass is made of lead, no natural buoyancy, and if he didn't teach me how to swim, I would sink and be forced to live at the bottom of the lake."

"You mean… *drown*?"

"Nah. Link says I'm indestructible and would survive"—I pointed straight down—"the deepest part of this lake." Out in front of my dock, the bottom sloped at a drastic rate. That was where my brother, Link, and I would have competitions for our rookie deep dives.

A great smile took over Crash's face. "I'm starting to believe your friend has that right." He looked at the water again. "Umm… where is he?"

Link had disappeared under the water again. "Picking up speed under the surface. You won't see him again. He has the lungs of a dolphin." Our dives had made Link one hell of a swimmer. My lungs had strengthened but not to Link's level.

"No, I mean your brother—"

I screamed as Link grabbed my foot while sneakily climbing the wooden ladder, laughing and shaking water from his hair. "I want some."

"Sex?" I teased Link.

"Not from you," Link answered with a disgust that was not necessarily pleasing to my ego.

I looked at Crash with a raised eyebrow. With perfect timing, Crash announced, "Don't look at me. Link already shot me down."

Hysterically laughing, Link finished climbing up and sat next to a pizza box at my side. He reached in without being offered a slice. "Extra pepperoni? Whit! Trying to die at an early age?"

"Trying, but you won't let me. Hey, if it's so bad, why are you moaw'n down?"

Speaking around a mouthful of pizza, Link said, "Because if you're going, I'm going with you."

I winked at Crash. "See? My weakest link."

"How old are you, Crash?" asked Link.

"Twenty." Crash spoke on the quiet side.

"Huh, my girl is only seventeen."

Crash winced. "Does an abundance of immaturity help?"

Links eyebrows furrowed. "Hasn't been determined yet."

Crash laughed. "Are you guys together—like always? You sound alike."

I was offended. "One: I don't sound like him."

"Two," added Link with his naturally deep voice, "I don't sound like a girl."

Crash shook his head. "No. Not voice. Your wording."

Link and I looked at each other and shrugged, simultaneously saying, "That's true."

We all laughed when Crash yelled, "See?"

Crash, Link, and I sat on the dock as the sun set, polishing off the pizzas. Crash watched Link trace a weathered carving in the dock. "What's that?"

"A symbol that reminds me of one of my favorite places. The water," answered Link with a smirk at me.

"Why the mischievous grin?" asked Crash.

Pointing at the symbol, I answered. "Because this homemade artwork pissed my mother off!"

Link and I burst out laughing. He struggled to breathe. "Damn! I thought that woman was going to have me arrested for 'ruining' her precious expensive dock, which she *never* takes the time to enjoy." Link rolled his eyes.

"And *why* is this so funny?"

Link and I looked at each other. "Because it pissed her off!"

Crash nodded. "Ah, I see. One point for the team against pain-in-the-ass parents."

"Exactly!" exclaimed Link. "Juvenile, I know but—"

"But it sure felt good!" I hollered, feeling the gratification all over again. Link and I high-fived.

Link inhaled deeply. "Well, I'm out. Got a date with Constance tonight." He kissed my cheek before pushing off the dock and splashing into the water. When he reemerged, he smiled up at me. "You'll probably be asleep before I get home, so good night, baby."

He was telling me I would not be receiving his blinking light. "Good night. Love you."

Link winked. "Love you too, girl. See ya, Crash."

"Peace out."

After Link swam home, playfully yelling, "Swimmer's cramp!" about his belly being full of pizza, Crash and I talked more.

"And your favorite song?" I asked.

"'Devil's Got My Secret' by Mieka Pauley."

"Who?"

"A singer I saw live once and felt she was singing… *my* life."

"What's the song about?"

He whispered, "A secret," then pulled out his cell phone and played a haunting song.

"The Devil's got my secret…

He swore he'd never tell…
I left it for safe-keeping…
I'll pick it up in Hell…"

Chills ran up my spine while I looked at the young man lost in a memory that seemed all consuming. I'll never forget hearing the music echoing over the lake and feeling how Crash had a story he wasn't willing to share… and how a part of me knew I didn't want him to.

When the same black car came to retrieve Crash, I didn't see the driver through the dark-tinted windows, and again, I didn't ask. Instead, I waved goodbye and walked into my home, set the alarm, and knocked on my brother's door with a glass of milk in my hand. I thought of the haunting lyrics, realizing we all have a secret in Hell. After not even a peep, I crawled into bed and passed out with a full belly, a sense of closeness with Crash, and a little unexpected life in my heart.

CHAPTER FOUR

Risks and Rage

REHEARSALS WERE MERCILESS FOR THE rest of the week. My instructors worked vigorously with me, giving excellent pointers on timing with my senior project. *"...and hold, hold, NOW. Yes, beautiful, Whitney. Feel the difference?"* They tweaked my emotional presentation and fine-tuned the routine.

I was exhausted and almost canceled skating, but when Crash texted saying he couldn't wait to see me, I mustered up the energy to play.

At six o'clock sharp, a yellow Lotus pulled into my driveway. The fancy automobile explained Mr. Lickable not being impressed with my living quarters. "Nice ride," I told him as he opened his passenger door for me. "I could have just ridden with Link."

"I pick up my own girl." Crash's eyes darkened.

Being completely stubborn, I leaned my back against his fancy car, refusing to get in. "I'm not your girl." I crossed my arms. I didn't allow my parents to rule my world, and I surely wasn't going to let anyone else. I demanded my independence whenever possible.

Crash stepped right up to me, chest to—well, he was approximately 5' 10" —so chest to ribcage. "Not yet." Then he waited, as if daring me to deny it.

I demanded my heart stop hammering in excitement. I forced my lungs to act as if they weren't gasping for air at having this divine creature so close to me. My eyes stared into his to see who would break first.

Crash grinned sexily, as if he appreciated my fight but had fight of his own. "Bad, bad Franky."

I stood my ground.

He slowly took a step back and gestured for me to get into the car.

I stood my ground.

Crash chuckled. "Okay, you win. You won't be my girl… until *you* say."

I wanted to scream, "Now! I'll be your girl right this very second!" but had to make a point and climbed into his vehicle, acting as if I were unaffected.

Pulling into the skating rink's side parking lot, I noticed Link's car so we parked next to it. Then I saw Link and Constance in his car doing what they *constantly* did—sucking face. "Oh God, here we go again." I grabbed my worn, black leather mailbag.

Crash chuckled at my dismay. "Not into some PA?"

I couldn't stop my eye roll. "It's not the public part, it's the—"

"Are you jealous? Link more to you than you say he is?"

I winced at such a thought. "Ew, gross. Not one ounce in my body wants… *his*."

Seeming convinced with my honest reaction, Crash laughed. "Note taken." He turned off the engine.

"It's just… well, it's the *all-the-time* thing of it."

Crashed leaned forward so his arms could rest over his steering wheel, his eyes studying me. "You've never dated someone you've wanted to kiss a lot?"

I thought about it. I hadn't really dated anyone worth mentioning. And it never lasted more than a date or so. I couldn't fathom why, nor did it bother me. I had Link, Ford, and Harlan. "No, I guess not." After another thought, I asked, "Do you think that means he *really* likes her? I mean, does Link always being down her throat mean he truly *does* love her?" My fingers fidgeted with my mailbag's zipper.

Crash looked past me out his passenger window and into Link's for a moment. "I don't know. I've never been in love… and to be completely honest, I've only kissed a girl in attempt to persuade her to have sex with me. I've never dated a girl I couldn't get enough of."

With inquisitive eyes, I looked at him. "Why do I believe you?"

"Because you seem to have a bullshit meter that's in top working order. Besides, what guy would tell a girl *that* to trick her?" Blue eyes sparkled in the dark, tempting me.

"I take it you're not trying to have sex with me? Don't forget about my bullshit reader."

He laughed a deep burst, and it seemed so *real.* "Won't lie, Franky. I have pictured it every day since I've met you, but my single desire has changed into multiple and, well, has me a little baffled."

"Baffled in a *good* way?"

With his keys in his hand, Crash looked at me. "I'm not sure." He pointed to the slobbering fishes. "What if I end up like him?"

I looked at Link and his desperate need for Connie the Terrible, completely understanding Crash's fear. "It would be scary for someone to have such control over you."

He softly said, "Again, I don't know. Never happened to me before."

With my mind made up and my heart picking up its pace, I faced Crash. "Okay. How about we don't kiss till we're sure it's worth the risk?"

He smirked. "Isn't there a saying, 'great plans lead to victory'?"

I shrugged nonchalantly, but my blood raced through my veins with excitement. "Don't know, but it sounds intelligent."

"And we *are* intelligent." Mr. Lickable leaned toward me, his breathing pattern picking up a few notches.

"Two of the smartest," I replied, meeting him in the middle, struggling for air.

"Wanna kiss?" Urgency and need shone in his eyes.

"Yes," I hungrily answered, and we quickly moved our mouths toward one another. I could feel the heat beaming off his lips and was desperate for their touch—

KNOCK, KNOCK, KNOCK!

Crash and I jumped then looked outside my passenger window. What we saw was Link's shit-eating grin. What we *heard* was, "What the hell are you two doing?"

Link sucks!

As I opened the passenger door with irritation my best friend could have read from a thousand miles away, I growled. "Don't you have spit to swallow somewhere?"

The bastard just kept grinning as I got out of the Lotus. "Looks like I'm not the only swapper. Hmm, Miss Whitney?" I growled again and slammed the door then walked between cars toward the skating rink's entrance.

That made him laugh. "Ahhh, all right. I pissed you off. I'm sorry. Come back, baby!"

"Hey, hey, hey." Crash caught up to me and gently grabbed my arm to stop my childish behavior. "Why are you so angry?"

I stopped walking and crunched my eyebrows in confusion. "Uh, I don't really know."

Crash's smile was kind. He softly touched my cheek. "I see that."

Now I was embarrassed. "What is my deal?"

Crash slowly dropped his hand from my face and eyed Link in thought. After a moment, his gaze met mine again, and he smirked. "You ready?"

"For what?"

To my utter amazement, rough, tough Crash started expertly rattling his whole body while singing "Shake it Off" by Taylor Swift. It is one of my most ridiculous memories of that young man. And one of my best.

Probably needless to say, I howled in gut-busting laughter and forgot about whatever had me so agitated.

Opening the skating rink doors, we heard "Like a Virgin" playing over the speakers. I grabbed Crash's hand without thinking and dragged him to the rink. "Hurry! You'll miss it! It's even worse than your T-Swizzle impersonation!" As we ran, I felt his fingers intertwine with mine. I didn't know all my senses could occupy such a small part of my body, but every bit of my concentration lingered around his simple touch. I was afraid my hand would start to sweat in lust as we approached the rink of skaters.

After getting his first glimpse of idiocy, Crash grabbed his exasperated mouth and uttered, "Oh, sweet mother of God. You weren't joking, Franky. He's got me beat."

My dear friend, Ford, was on his skate wheels touching his nipples, rolling backward, with his eyes closed, his head swaying, and shamelessly singing—as loud as possible, "Like a Virgin." At that sight, I was sure the kid *was* a virgin because no girl in her right mind would—I take that back. It was adorable, and his fun way of life was a total chick magnet.

Link walked up to us. "Makes you want to scrub your eyeballs with bleach, don't it?"

Crash numbly replied, "I was thinking more along the lines of acid."

"And the girls keep lining up for him. Amazing." Constance smirked. Not even she was unaffected by the comical scene.

"I'm shocked he hasn't been kicked out yet," said Crash, still in awe.

"His uncle owns the joint," I explained. "Want some popcorn?"

Crash forcefully pulled his eyes away from the train wreck. "How can you think of food after such a—"

Just then Ford passed us by again, still singing of course. Harlan proudly followed, videoing with his phone and announcing, "I'm feeling a YouTube video montage in the making, people! Who wouldn't watch this shit?"

Crash looked at me in horror as he realized the world was about to be subjected to a sight that would change the eighties forever and agreed to the much-needed escape. "Extra butter?"

Eating my popcorn, I saw ink peaking out from under Crash's charcoal T-shirt. One word was on his right bicep. "So how'd you get the nickname *Crash*, Crash?"

He looked down, looking almost ashamed. "Uh, just a nickname that stuck."

Not wanting him uncomfortable about an issue he clearly had with his permanent marking, I slid my popcorn bag under his nose. "I'll share with you."

It worked. Crash looked up. "But Link said you never share with anyone."

"Maybe I don't consider you just anyone."

He took a deep breath and a piece of popcorn. "You're getting harder to resist, Franky."

"Too bad I can't say the same about you."

Crash laughed. "I do nothin' for you, huh?"

"Not. A. Thing."

"You lying to me, Franky girl?"

Yes. "Not my style."

He seductively leaned over the table in between us. I didn't move. "What if I kissed you as a test?"

"It's a free country," I casually replied, desperate to feel his mouth on mine.

He stared at my wanting lips. "Yes… it sure is." He sat back in his seat without so much as a peck!

My jaw dropped. "That's it?"

He nonchalantly took a sip of his Coke. "What's the matter?"

My eyes squinted in judgment. "You know *exactly* what's wrong."

"I thought I had no effect on you, Franky."

I sat back, practically pouting. "You don't. I just... *forgot*. That's all."

Crash shrugged his proud-to-have-affected-me shoulders. "Besides, we're going to make sure it's worth the risk, right?"

We both had already silently made that decision in the car, but apparently he wanted more proof, so I smirked. *Challenge accepted.* "Before this night is over, Mr. Lickable, I'll have you completely and totally convinced."

"Mr. Lickable?"

Shit. "I said that out loud, huh?"

Crash's ego practically grew before me as he beamed. "Why, yes you did, Franky."

We had a blast. Crash was definitely inexperienced with skates but was a good sport every time he landed on his ass. And he was a good sport as we skated around him, laughing unmercifully at his humiliation, Harlan videoing every mishap. An eighties classic, "True Colors" by Cyndi Lauper, came on, so I shyly asked Crash, "Wanna couple skate?"

His phenomenal grin appeared. "You going to take hold of my hand again?"

I instantly remembered grabbing his hand when we'd first arrived. My hand quickly warmed in anticipation and need, but I smarted off. "Can't handle a girl who knows what she wants?"

Crash leaned to my ear. "I like aggressive women." He shocked me when he took hold of my hand and then, this time, kissed it ever so gently. Our eyes slowly met. Then our hearts slowly met. It was as if he magically captured any of my attention that may have not been all his. It was a needing-no-words-to-explain-it kind of connection. I felt we were two souls running from secrets that chased and taunted our pain. Crash and I both regularly teased and played around with the people surrounding us simply to disguise, well, our *disguise*.

A spark kept trying to ignite in my saddened heart, and I felt as if I had known Crash all my life and that I always would. He was a temptation I couldn't deny.

With normal shoes back on, hand in hand, Crash and I headed for his car, wanting to explore what was spreading like wildfire between us. We had left early, making it clear to everyone we wanted to have dinner alone.

Somehow, subconsciously, we both knew we were trying to leave so much behind, trying to run as fast as we could so reality would allow us one of the happiest times—no, the happiest time—in our overwhelming lives.

"Where did you come from, Franky?"

We got to his car. "Would you believe from the Heavens above?"

He pulled me to him with such tenderness it healed a part of my soul I didn't realize was damaged. His strong hand ran through my hair as if to just get me closer to him. We were face to face, only the remnant of distant streetlamps glowed. He whispered to me with such emotion, I knew he wasn't trying to fool me. "You make me wish my life was different, Franky."

"Are you saying I'm worth the risk?" I touched his scar.

"More." The hand holding my head let go and grabbed my hand to stop my touch. His eyes saddened. "I'm saying… you make me want to forget." He stopped and stared at my hand, as if scared to share his truth. "You make me want to drift away from it all."

I knew we weren't talking physical move but a mental escape. It was as if he understood my constant inner marathon. I loved the feeling of not being alone with the never-ending mental race. I didn't know what his 'it' was, but I pulled my hand from his and wrapped my arm around his neck. I whispered my wish. "Take me when you go."

Sounding vulnerable, he asked, "What if the destination is not drift-worthy?"

"Crash—" I wanted him to know I was making a vow, even if it was a crazy thing to do, even if it showed my age and immaturity. "Setting sail with you —wherever the wind takes us—is where I want to go… Harold."

His expression softened. "Wow. I finally like my real name."

Our lips slowly descended to one another, barely touching, but it was enough to feel like an awakening.

My innocent, beautiful awakening morphed into a nightmare as Link shoved Crash away from me. "You're a liar!" he yelled. "I learned about your nickname, *Crash*."

Completely stunned, I yelled back, "Link! What the hell has gotten into you?"

The same black car that usually shadowed Crash came speeding toward us. The driver and passenger doors opened, and two huge men who looked to be prime examples of well-dressed thugs stepped out.

Ford, Harlan and Constance, still in skates, rolled up to Link. Their bodies awkwardly wobbled over rocks, trying to stay off their asses.

"Please, baby..."

"Link, damn it..."

"These guys are packing..."

Packing?

But my best friend had no fear when it came to protecting me. Apparently, Crash understood this too and put his hands up to halt his suspicious approaching company. I looked at the boy I'd just promised my heart to. "Crash? What's going on?"

"Yeah, *Crash*," Link sneered. "Why don't you tell her?"

Again, Ford, Harlan, and Connie begged in the background, their words not penetrating my burning ears. Link would not be silenced. He just yelled, "Do you know who you're about to crush?" His finger pointed me out to Crash.

Crash's eyebrows were creased as he tried to explain something I didn't understand. "I won't let it effect her. Link! She won't be apart of it; I swear it! I'll find a way."

I stood in between Crash and Link. "A part of what?" But I got nowhere because Link was beyond agitated. He was furious! His body shook, and he hollered at Crash. "No! Do you *know* her last name?"

Crash's bleak expression was alarming. "No. We chose to leave family drama out—"

Link screamed, "Summers! Her last name is Summers!"

Crash froze and then went pale. Crash finally looked at me and whispered my last name. "Summers." Then he whispered a name I hadn't heard in five years. "Timothy." After the first year, it was simply too painful to hear, so my friends stopped saying it.

"That's right," said Link and then finished with a name I knew well. "Thompson. Or should I say, Junior?"

Thompson? I was ashamed I hadn't put it together before, but truly, how could I have known? It was as if my cloud of bliss had been lifted only to present the hell I knew I could never run from, no matter how hard I tried. As I looked from the dark mysterious car, to the men who occupied it, and back to Crash—the young man who was truly the bad boy mamas warn you about—and put all the facts together, my heart broke.

Crash had so much sympathy in his eyes it terrified me. He knew. He knew exactly who I was. He knew exactly what his family had done to mine, and somehow I could feel him care. It didn't change my past though. No amount of his empathy would.

My knees felt like Jell-O, causing me to fall backward into Link. Crash reached out to help catch me, but I pulled my hand away, not wanting anyone of his kind touching me. Never would I want the son of a drug lord touching me, especially when the heroin they sold was the heroin that had ended my brother's life.

Link held my back to his chest with his arm protectively around me as he warned Crash and his company. "Stay away from her. Do you hear me?"

Crash stepped forward. "Wait, she's little t—"

I gasped and met Crash's eyes, knowing he knew something sacred about my brother as I was being handed off to Ford and Harlan. Link faced off against Crash and his two questionable friends. "Don't come near her. I'm not like her parents! I will use every connection my family has to have your whole fucked up organization buried like it deserves!"

I felt dazed and sucked back into a time, a memory I'd fought so hard to escape. I guess you never escape the loss of a sibling you adored and looked up to. Link wouldn't have been my hero if my brother had still been alive. I'd been Tim's treasure. He would always call me his little…

"Wait!" I tried to interrupt to find out how Crash knew my personal nickname, but Link, undeterred, guardedly pushed me behind him once again.

"Franky—"

Link growled. "Stay. Away. She is not Franky. She is nothing to you. Ford, get my girls out of here now."

As Ford led Constance and me away, Harlan stayed behind, flanking Link, and I watched Crash. He had his hands up, telling Link he would not follow, to calm down, but he watched me intently. There was a message in those blue eyes. They were trying to tell me something. Something I had to know.

CHAPTER FIVE

Fire and Glue

On our silent ride home, Link explained how someone we knew from school had approached him at the skating rink after Crash and I had left, and that's how he'd learned about Crash. Link asked over and over again if I was okay. My friend knew I was lying when I said I was fine, but he let me go into my empty home so I could be alone.

I knocked on my brother's closed bedroom door, which was never open because my parents had preferred it that way. With no answer—like every night—I called out to him. "Tim?"

No answer. I finally opened the door and walked inside.

Nothing had been disturbed. The room was exactly how it had been left. It was as if Tim had just gone to a friend's for a long weekend. But he hadn't. He had left for good, and I missed him dearly.

I crawled into my brother's bed, wishing I could still smell him, wishing I had been old enough to understand everything that went so tragically wrong when I was eleven. Timothy had been seventeen, my age at the present, when one too many needles became too much for him.

My parents didn't speak of the details with me. I had to get that from the media.

"Todd Summers is sharing in the grief of losing a child to the overwhelming drug problem in our town… His son has been laid to rest… Summers says, 'I think it is time to take a stand… and fight for our town.'"

I was proud. My father had been trying to make something of my brother's death. That's why I was confused when my father's publicity people decided to seize the moment and jump aboard, and so did what was left of this broken family. My mother more than willing—me not so much. I had no time to catch up emotionally. It was as if my mother felt Tim's death was just what my father needed to lift him politically, not the tragic loss it truly was. And for some unknown reason, the sight of me agitated her more than usual. There was no mourning, just strategic planning during many hushed meetings in my father's home office. I only wanted my father's embrace and believed he would give it to me as soon as he found the time.

I was young but old enough to feel shame at my mother's actions and lack of caring for my brother and myself. If I tried to speak out, speak of Tim or my aching heart, my mother would become hostile, quickly shutting me down with harsh words. *"He is gone, Whitney! Why must you say his name? This is a very important time for your father. Stop ruining it with your constant dribbling."*

Dribbling. She actually used that word to describe my wanting to speak of my deceased brother. To avoid her cruelty, I learned to fake my emotions. How could I not hate her? How could I ever see her as a mother and not the raving bitch she'd proved, over and over, to be?

Because of my brother's death, drugs disgusted me. That meant Crash now disgusted me too. With my nerves on edge, my cell phone ringing made me jump. "Uh, hello?"

"Hello, dear. Was your evening pleasant?"

Once again, it was time to pretend to be the daughter she wanted, not the one she had. Confiding in her about the tortuous night I'd just had would've been wasting my breath. "Yes, Mother." I walked to my brother's back window, waiting for Link's blink. "Is Father available to talk?"

"No, he is not. You know he is busy, dear."

Link's light did not say good night.

"Yes, I know."

I lay back down, hugging my brother's pillow. "I'm sure Father will call when he has a free moment."

The next morning, I woke in my own bed. I didn't remember switching, but I did remember Crash's blue eyes in the parking lot the night before, trying to tell me something. Crash being the first person I thought of in the morning disturbed and disorientated me. I didn't know what part he'd played in my brother's death, but I was sure he was guilty. Therefore, no matter how much my heart was trying to remind me of the first interest I'd had in ages in the male gender, I told my heart to kiss my ass. I refused to be some tragic case who fell for her enemy. Crash might have been close to my age, therefore possibly not directly to blame, but I wasn't the heroine in *Romeo and Juliet*. I stubbornly reminded myself I was Whitney, and I had other things to focus on, like my Tender West dance audition.

I turned up the central house stereo so it echoed in every room. Desperate to leave behind my ugly funk, I let my body move to release what I didn't want to feel inside. I lied to myself after my shower and told myself I had washed away the old memories I'd learned to run from. Then I danced all the way down my staircase in complete denial of the lingering pain in my soul. I tried to convince myself I was absolutely uninjured as I sang while cooking eggs in a sizzling pan.

I tossed them in a bowl with salsa, still moving my body, forcing the search for inner comfort. I got so caught up in dancing, my eggs were left untouched on the counter while I lied to myself some more, saying I had found freedom in the music. Modern dancing and my distress became one.

Our extensive living room had long been my personal dance floor. Extending my legs high with the precision I was known for was almost freeing to my detained spirit. True emotions fought to escape the cage I'd placed them in. My hands banged on my chest, expressing the need to release my pent-up anguish. They also expressed my desperate need to suppress my despair. My body had talent to exude the emotion of any song, but it was confused by this internal battle. Before I knew it, I was lying on the floor gasping for air. It was apparent that there were some things I couldn't dance away.

When I faced that I had lost the war, I screamed out my frustration. "WHY?"

The knock at my sliding glass door had me jumping to my feet. It was Link, and he was wet. For the first time ever, I had forgotten about our swim. I opened the slider shamefully. "I'm sorry."

"He got to you."

It wasn't a question. It was a statement the dancing Link had just witnessed confirmed. I threw him a towel and defiantly marched back to my kitchen. "I don't want to talk about it."

I grabbed my bowl of eggs but was still too upset to eat them. I offered the bowl to Link. He agitatedly took the white porcelain dish and set it back onto the counter I leaned against and then got really close to my face. I felt his breath on my flushed face. "You have to stay away from him."

My eyes met his, and I growled. "No shit, Sherlock."

"He's dangerous, Whit."

I couldn't understand my anger toward my best friend, but I argued anyway. "Why are you so convinced I'm going to see him again?"

"Because you are as stubborn as they come, and as much as that is a quality I usually adore about you, this time, it will get you hurt."

I screamed in his face. "Too late! I'm already hurt!"

Link's eyes closed as he rested his weight on his hands on each side of me, trapping me against my mother's imported marble counters. "Shit... I'm sorry. I—I wanted your first love to be—"

I pushed him off me. "I don't *love* him." I walked away.

"Maybe not in the conventional adult way that we've been so pleasantly lectured about," he said, following me out of the kitchen with agitation laced in his voice, "but we teenagers can fall hard and fast." He grabbed my shoulders and turned me, forcing me to face him again. "It's the closest thing we understand to love." As my eyes watered against my will, his voice softened. "And it can sting as if we have been stabbed by a dull, rusty knife."

I fell into my friend, sharply feeling the demise he'd just spoken of. Link held me with much-needed affection. After a few silent moments, I whispered in tears. "I fell for him, Link."

Link slowly rocked me back and forth. "I know, baby. I know."

Link convinced me to still have our morning swim. I found myself in the middle of the lake, mentally drained. Treading water that felt colder than usual, he asked, "You okay?"

I looked around the glassy water and at the nature in between the four houses on the lake and tried to relax but I felt—I felt—

"Do you ever feel like you don't *belong*?"

Link mirrored me, treading water as it dripped from his wet dark hair. "Yes. Lately, even more so."

"Care to elaborate?"

He inhaled. My eyes followed his heavy exhale as it caused faint ripples in the water. "I'm slowly but surely learning nothing is ever what it seems." He went quiet.

Seeing how he was not delving deeper, I asked, "Do your new findings have something to do with the dark circles you have under your eyes?"

Link never looked drained. It was as if, that day, he suffered because I was suffering.

"No," he said, with exhaustion that tried to sound happy. "They're because I *literally* needed to see my Whitney."

For a second, I thought of teasing him, claiming not to be his, but the truth was, I had always been Link's. "I take it you don't plan on elaborating on that either?"

His blue eyes looked directly into mine, and I thought he might just open up. Instead, Link lightly grinned. "Want a ride home?"

I nodded because I knew him well. Conversation was over. And if I knew anything about Link, he always had a good reason for ending it. So my arm went around his neck as I lay on his back and accepted my piggyback ride home with my head gently resting on his. His warm skin stole away the chill that had been taking root.

Monday, still feeling depleted, I caught a ride with Link to school. Ford, Harlan, and Constance met us at his car. Connie walked up to me as I got out and softly asked me, "Are you okay?"

I looked at her, not with annoyance as usual, but with an honest question because she came and sat quietly with me, Link, Ford, and Harlan on Sunday. They all didn't want me to be alone. "Why are you being so nice to me?"

She looked at the ground and whispered, "Because I have been hurt too… That is why I cherish Link so much."

Her sincerity was so touching that all my ill feelings for her melted away. It happened so abruptly that I literally felt our past nonsense evaporate, making room for emotions that were so much more critical. And that was it—the end of my constant Connie-hating masquerade. We now had two common deep bonds: heartache and love for a wonderful young man named Link. It was also the first time I could acknowledge that I envied her. Connie had chosen someone honest and caring. She chose the good guy while I chased trouble as I if had no sense.

During first period as I sat at an old *Little House on the Prairie* desk, my phone vibrated.

I need to talk to you

Completely stunned into a motionless, breathless state, I sat there as if I might never move again. The first moment none of my closest friends were around, Crash had contacted me. I felt violated because there was a part of me I was beginning to hate: a deep part of me named desire. And that desire was becoming something I despised because, even without wanting to, I had gratitude that Crash had reached out to me, even though he'd been warned *not* to by Link. Somehow there was comfort in the knowing Crash could be suffering as I was.

I typed:

How do you know about Tim's nickname for me?

My phone vibrated again.

Come outside.

Why?

He only replied:

I'm behind the art building.

Even though it was borderline idiotic, I headed out my school's back door with a bathroom pass in hand. Unanswered questions, deep-rooted concerns, and an unacknowledged yearning were in charge of my actions. The only thing giving me an ounce of pride was the anger boiling as I realized Crash *assumed* I would come to him. That anger grew as I realized he was indeed correct. I was coming to him.

Ready to explode all over *Harold*, I marched outside and stomped down the sidewalk made of historic bricks toward the woods, until I heard, "You're cute when you lie about your profession, and you're even cuter when you're pissed."

He was trying to lighten the mood with his sly play—his disguise—but I heard in his voice that he knew it wouldn't work. Never try and bullshit a bullshitter. I spun to him with my finger pointed, ready to accuse, but when I saw him leaning against the wall with the sun dancing with his ice-blue eyes, I froze again.

Crash had seemed so attractive to me, but knowing the truth, I saw him in a different light, and I didn't care. That was when I knew I was in serious trouble—serious danger of losing myself to the worst of all the young men I could've fallen for.

Maybe my unwanted desire was written all over my face because Crash's demeanor suddenly changed, and he pushed his muscular body off the wall. "This is not one-sided, is it?"

Brown hair gently caressed a face that maybe not every girl had dreamed of, but I knew I had. The scar above his left eyebrow might have had some young girls wincing. Not me. And his freshly bruised cheek had me caring about who had dared to hurt him.

"Is it, Franky?" he repeated, sounding timid.

The disfiguring scar on his bottom lip might have turned some away. It had me touching it, wanting to kiss there, to show him his imperfections made no difference to me, and I wanted to punish whoever had brought Crash harm.

Crash leaned into my touch, his eyes closing. With his body close to mine, he whispered, "Is it?"

Feeling his body heat blend with mine, I wanted to tell him I was still with him, but instead, the bold tattoo on his right bicep peeking out from under his short-sleeved T-shirt had me asking once again, "Why Crash? Why that nickname?"

His eyes opened. After some silence he said, "I don't want to lie to you."

"Then don't."

He took one step back as if he already knew his answer was going to push me over the cliff I was barely balancing on. "My nickname is because… I'm who you are to come to… when your high ends and you… crash."

Thinking him wise to have backed away, I growled with hurt and disgust, "My brother crashed in the worst way possible. Why didn't you save him, *Crash*?" He tried to talk, but his prior answer had my heart plummeting away from sincere affections. I put my hand up to demand he stop. Before my tears fell, I told him, "Don't ever come near me again," and walked away from the only guy I had ever knowingly wanted to run to.

The only way I can explain how Crash innocently consumed my every thought is to describe what it is like to go thirsty—dying-in-the-desert kind of thirst. I would have sold my soul to drink from him, but I refused to taint the memory of my brother, so I let my hate build instead.

I ignored every text and became annoyed every time Crash mysteriously appeared. He followed me, keeping his distance, into many stores or restaurants. No friends seemed to notice. They all seemed to believe the short-lived fling was over. They had all forgotten the night I met the one who would remind me of my brother's nonexistence and steal a piece of me at the same time. I guess my usual denial reaction to trauma had my friends thinking I had once again healed in record time.

On one occasion, sitting at a table in the ice cream shop, Link looked over his shoulder out the front window. "What are you looking at?"

I was looking at Crash standing across the street watching me, but I licked my one-scoop chocolate cone and dryly replied, "Ab-so-lute-ly *nothing*." Not even a car passing between us broke Crash's stare.

Link casually texted on his phone. "How's your routine coming along?"

My dance instructor had been working my ass off—literally. That was why I was guilt-free while eating ice cream. Rehearsals were relentless. "Like it's a part of my soul." My life was relentless too.

"That's my girl," said Link, clueless of my inner torment. Within moments, Crash seemed to be reading his cell as he stormed off. *I guess he had to save another druggy from his or her* crash.

On another occasion, I was pumping gas when Crash's Lotus pulled up behind my car. Getting out of his assumingly drug-paid automobile, he looked ready to beg. "Talk to me."

I faced him with rage. "Did my brother die from an overdose of your father's product?"

He inhaled deeply. "Yes, but—"

He stopped as I pushed passed him to reattach the gas nozzle to its holder. "You. Make. Me. Sick."

I closed my gas cap and got into my car to race away from the only person I wanted to race to.

After I learned who Crash was, I knew what song I wanted for my audition: "How" by Chasing Jonah, an indie rock project I loved. This nostalgic song touched me deeply, and Crash fit every word. Time passed in a blur with how hard I worked—how hard I sunk every emotion into practice. Before I knew it, the audition had arrived, and I took my place on stage.

The converted church at my school had rows of seats I couldn't see beyond the powerful stage lights. I could barely see the judges silently waiting.

I took a deep inhale for courage. The music began:

"You stare me down like you're trying to get me to talk
You're cutting through my heart-built roadblocks
You drew me in with the colors of your soul
I gave in and slipped you some control…"

As the music built, my soul set fire. *"How…"*

I let go. *"How…"*

I stopped holding back and jumped through the air as if I were fighting to break free from an invisible prison. I rolled around on the floor begging the earth to heal the unhealable.

"I was worried about the sword in your hand
Till I realized you're fighting the very battle I am
I couldn't gauge how close you were to home
So I took a hit and watched my heart go…"

For the brief moments Crash and I'd had, I'd felt as if he was the magical glue reattaching me. With every movement, it was as if I sang with my body… to him. My heart pleaded for Crash to glue every broken piece back together.

"How…"

Every physical movement had emotions on such a level that I forgot about the judges, the ones who were there to choose. I danced to save my soul.

When the song ended, I stood at the center of the stage motionless, except for my exerted breathing. I was stunned with how far my mind had strayed and how much my heart had taken over my body. I guess the judges had strayed with me because they stared at me, completely speechless.

Mentally coming back to the auditorium, I slowly looked to the wings. Standing there, with an exasperated expression, was Crash.

He knew. Crash knew I'd just danced… for him.

I quietly thanked the silent judges for their consideration and time, and exited to where Crash waited for me. As I passed him to change into my school uniform, he whispered, "You're beautiful." He followed my sweating body out to a school hallway, but I refused to stop. He suddenly grabbed my arm, pressed me up against the wall, and stood with his body to mine. We both panted for air. With his jaw rigid, he quietly growled, "Tell me I'm still not alone in this! Ignore me if you will, but don't fucking lie to yourself."

His fingers touching me and his body so close had me finally caving to my desires. I shrieked, "You're still not alone! I shouldn't, but damn it I want you!"

I was about to scream that I hated myself for my weakness, but I couldn't because his hands grasped my face in a rush. His open mouth came to devour mine. I was pitifully thankful to finally be forced to drink the water I so desperately craved. Face to face, breath to breath.

"Is everything okay here?"

Crash and I looked at the teacher who came from his classroom after my vocal explosion. I was still out of breath from my audition and from the need to feel more of Crash's touch. I believe Mr. Roberts misunderstood my body's state for fear because he looked Crash up and down. "Are you a new student here?"

Crash looked back to me, whispered, "Thank you for not lying," and took off, leaving me emotionally off-kilter. I had no idea where we stood. I had no clue if I was strong enough to handle Crash. I only felt lost and ashamed for wanting him.

The teacher yelled, "Hey! Come back here!" but Crash was around a corner and probably off school property in a heartbeat.

"Do you know him?" The teacher's words pulled me from drowning, all-consuming sorrow.

"No," I said in agony. "No I do not."

It wasn't a lie. I did not know the young man who violently possessed me.

CHAPTER SIX

Truth and Trust

LINK'S AUNT HAD SUDDENLY FALLEN ill, so his father had them on a flight with no notice. My best friend seemed distraught to be leaving me as he called on the way to the airport. I chuckled to calm his nerves. "Breathe! I'm fine. Take care of your family. They come first. I understand that, Link."

"You—*you* come—" He stopped himself. "Shit!"

I heard his father in the background. "Reether, off the phone. Last warning." Mr. Jones's tone surprised me. He sounded highly agitated. So did Link when he muffled the phone to speak with his dad. "This is wrong! She's only seventeen!"

"Link? Who's only seventeen?"

"Uh," Link stuttered, "my, uh, cousin. And the family is, uh, making her watch over my aunt."

I understood his frustration. "Well, lucky for her you are on your way to take some weight off her shoulders."

Link blew out an exasperated breath. "Whit… I… I love you, girl."

The smile that appeared on my face came straight from my heart. "I love you too," I told him before hanging up. Sitting at the edge of my dock, I gazed up at his empty bedroom on the second floor, mirroring mine, and was saddened to know there would be no blinking good-night light tonight. Knowing he'd be back had me thinking about how lucky I was to have Link, someone to try to make up for the loss of my brother.

When he died, I couldn't gather the essential parts of my life force and reassemble them to become whole again. Dealing with my mother's cold ways were tolerable because of Link. That made him a hero of sorts.

Having a *true* hero is a lie. That fact had never been more evident than the day Timothy died, but you know the saying, *ignorance is bliss.* I wanted my ignorance back.

And that was Link.

He'd slid into the hero role and kept me from completely falling apart. In the quiet of the night, the importance of his very existence finally became clear. He was so… loyal. It was an odd word to use when describing a friend, but that was how I felt. Until that lonely night, I hadn't understood how much I counted—every day—on that allegiance.

Link always seemed two steps ahead when it came to my happiness. I wondered if he had me in the lake every morning on purpose. *Does he understand what this water means to me?* Did he understand the memories connected to the blue waters? Believing he did, indeed, know what he was doing had me reminiscing about when I was eight…

Timothy chuckled and teased me. "Stop whining and leap."

"I'm afraid."

He knelt next to me on the dock and pointed. "You see the blue waters?"

It was one body of water, but my brother always said *waters,* as if rebelling against his education because my parents' money was attached to it. Maybe my own rebellion was learned by example.

The rising sun shone off the beautiful water. "Yes."

He spoke with heart. "Picture me in that water, waiting to catch you. I will always be in those blue waters waiting for you, my little treasure."

My brother always had spoken to me as if my value—my worth—was only recognized by him, that he was the only one who truly cared. Maybe the way he viewed was the inspiration for my fight to think outside the box.

Because it was nighttime, I couldn't see the deep, clear, blue water, but I tried to imagine and feel the peace the water used to bring me. I tried to believe Tim was really waiting for me there. I felt comforted to know the water beneath my toes had once touched his. Who would ever have thought that after death, water could connect you to the one long gone?

The moon showed the shallow ripples, almost entrancing me until I heard someone in the grass walking toward me. I jerked to face the intruder. Crash quickly said, "It's just me."

"That's worse than an abductor or burglar. How'd you get past security?" I stood, extremely agitated with the intrusion.

"Security is just a façade when someone *really* wants in."

"Ah, not only have you been well trained in the art of selling drugs, but also to rob people of cherished items. Very reassuring."

He walked down my dock toward me. "I have no choice but to sell, and you're giving me no choice but to sneak into this compound like a damn criminal."

"A zebra can't change his stripes; nor can you, *Crash*. You are what you are."

"Jesus, Franky. Can you cut me some slack? Give me a chance—"

"Mr. Criminal, let me ask you this—did my brother have a chance?"

Crash's shoulders slumped. "No, but—"

"Take your talents elsewhere." I turned back to the water. "Please. Leave."

"Franky, I'm pleading with you to let me explain."

In a blur, I faced my enemy and yelled, "There is no explanation worthy of his death! You killed my brother!" And then, with all my might, with all that I had penned up for five years, I shoved his chest. Crash flew backward into the water.

Immediately, I felt regret. I had just corrupted my brother's blue waters with someone vile.

Crash's hands reached up, grabbed the edge of the dock, and he emerged with barely any effort. "I have something I have to tell you about your brother."

I ran. To hear him utter one more word about Timothy was stressing me to the point my throat felt like it was closing—crushing my windpipe, so I ran for my own survival.

"Damn it! Franky!" Crash's wet clothes sloshing grew louder behind me. "You WILL hear me!"

"No!" I screamed, but was tackled to the ground. I fought, but was forced to my back where Crash sat on my stomach, holding me down. I pushed at him until he captured my hands and pinned them above my head. Water from the lake dripped from him and soaked me through. He looked crazed. "I didn't kill him! I was fucking thirteen when he died! I loved him! He was a brother to me!"

Crash telling me with such conviction that he loved my brother ended my struggle. I stared up at the one I knew nothing about and realized I might have known nothing about my own brother. Knowing he was reaching me, that I was finally listening, Crash nodded. "Yes. My family may have been to blame—your family may have been to blame... but not me. When you lost your brother... I lost mine too. And once he was gone, I knew I would never know the one he spoke of—his little treasure."

It felt as though my brother blew through my soul. Someone who knew such a private nickname could never have been anyone Tim hadn't trusted. Tim only used this nickname when we were alone or with Link. For some reason, Timothy said our parents wouldn't "appreciate" it. Then he would chuckle. This meant the person sitting on top of me, trapping me, was someone my brother loved too. I wasn't alone.

His forehead rested to mine as tears spilled from my injured soul. I had so many questions, but couldn't gather traction to speak.

"I'm so sorry," Crash whispered. "He adored you."

Barely audible words escaped me. "I adored *him*... he was ripped from me... Why?"

"Something much bigger than us. Something you and I can never take on."

I growled up to the dangerous young man on top of me. "That is *not* what I want to hear! Give me something I—we *can* control."

That was the monumental moment when Crash crashed into me.

His lips devoured mine as if he had hungered all his life to eat me alive, and I didn't fight him. My mouth opened as I finally drank the water I'd so desired.

We lay facing each other in my backyard. "You ruined my cell phone," said a smirking Crash, as I traced my finger along another tattoo on his right arm.

I winced, remembering pushing him into the lake, drowning his phone. "Sorry." I ran my hand up to touch the scar above his eyebrow. As he always did, he removed my hand. He kissed my finger then held my hand gently, telling me not to push into territories he didn't want to think about.

"You're shaking," Crash whispered with concern in his eyes. The only warmth I felt was Crash, but it wasn't enough to ease my frightened heart. I worried about his painful past and... "I'm scared of what you have to tell me."

He affectionately kissed the tip of my nose. "Can I take you inside first?"

"Your words are going to change me, aren't they?"

"Yes."

I was surprised when Crash led me inside my house as if he had been there before. I was even more surprised when he guided me to the kitchen and got me a glass of milk. He held my hand as we slowly ascended my staircase. Crash looked at my brother's bedroom, but went to mine. I stood motionless and dumbfounded as he reached into my pajama drawer and pulled out my favorite set. Crash turned and faced me, looking shameful. I thought it was because he had obviously been spying on me, but it wasn't.

"As Tim… was dying… I made a promise to watch over you." He looked in my eyes and whispered, "I'm sorry… I was so young and couldn't—didn't know how to find you… but since the day I found out who you were, I have watched your every move."

"You… you… were with him when… he died?"

Crash usually looked tougher than nails, so it was terrifying to see his eyes swell. "Yes." He took my milk in exchange for my PJs.

Numbly, I walked into my bathroom with my PJs in hand. Numbly, I showered. Numbly, I dressed.

Walking out my bathroom, I expected Crash to be waiting, but he wasn't. I grabbed my milk off my dresser and found him in my brother's bedroom. Without facing me, Crash held up a T-shirt and a pair of Tim's sweatpants. "Do you mind?"

It was going to be difficult to see someone else in his clothing, but I whispered, "No."

Crash went into Tim's bathroom and changed while I emptied my glass. When he came out, he still wouldn't look at me. I didn't know why. "Tim's last words… his last wish was… for you to be safe in your bed… every night."

Thinking of how I'd woken in my own bed not knowing how I got there, my hand tried to cover my audible gasp. "You moved me the other night?"

Crash's fingers ran over Tim's football trophies. "I'm not a stalker. Your parents just have a shitty, overpriced security system."

I set my glass on Tim's nightstand. "How do you know how to get past it?"

He finally faced me. "I was raised by evil."

My legs gave out, so I sat on the ivory shag carpet, trying to breathe, trying to prepare myself for answers I knew I didn't want to hear. Crash sat in font of me and softly asked, "Can I hold your hands?"

I nodded, wanting, needing his touch, needing *him*.

"Are you close with your parents?"

I could barely hear my own truth. "No."

"Do you believe they are good?"

A tear slipped from my eye. It was a symbol of what money couldn't buy: humanity.

His fingers tightened on mine. "Me too. I want to believe they love me, but I believe my father's actions are led more by ego than anything else."

"Your mom?"

"Absently addicted to what my father sells."

Again, I nodded through the rawest conversation of my life. "Like my brother?"

Crash looked at me with more of the sympathy I'd seen in the skating rink's parking lot. It gave me an unearthly chill. "No," he answered. "Your brother was never addicted to any drug. Your brother, Tim, was murdered."

CHAPTER SEVEN

Fear and Friends

SOME THINGS YOU WILL NEVER be prepared to hear.

It was one thing to believe my brother had been sad and turned to drugs to heal—to run from pain. I didn't know where the pain was coming from or why there had been any pain at all, but as I got older and saw my mom for what she was …

"You are despicable!" my mother said to me in the restaurant's bathroom stall. Vomit still hung from my trembling chin as I stood weakly, leaning against the stall wall. The flu that had been going around my elementary school had arrived in my body with a vengeance.

Mother wiped at my dress, trying to remove my dinner that refused to stay down, while lecturing me. "All I asked was for you to behave for your father's important dinner meeting, but no, you must be the center of attention, as usual."

The knock on the ladies' bathroom door only agitated my mother further, but she sang out with fake glee, "We'll be right out."

"It's just me. She okay?"

I was so fatigued that my brother's voice brought tears to my eyes.

My mother threw the small towel to the ground. "Let him care for your mess." She stormed out of the stall. "She smells. Get. Her. Home."

The woman and womb from which I came left me again.

I heard shuffles of shoes, then the bathroom door locked again. Timothy mumbled, "She warned you she was getting sick, you cold bitch."

My stall door swung open, and I looked up from the floor I'd slid to. Seeing my brother was like seeing, well, like seeing a real-life hero. I wanted my father to fill this role, and I knew he would—as soon as he had time.

Tim grinned. "Hey, little T. Ready to blow this joint?" He chuckled. "No pun intended." He carefully scooped me up.

"Timothy? Did I ruin Daddy's dinner meeting?"

"It's impossible to sabotage an already sinking ship."

He had just turned fifteen, but he spoke with the wisdom of a thirty-five-year-old.

Since my mother caused me constant anguish, I assumed she was to blame for Tim's drug abuse. So I ran, acted happy, always looked for fun so I wouldn't turn to drugs and numb myself. A part of me now wished I *had* accepted a substance. It might have made this easier to hear.

"Your father got... caught up in a business transaction with the wrong people."

I pulled his hands. "What people?"

He shook his head. He wasn't going to share. "Just people my father has been caught up with for longer than I've been alive."

"Other drug dealers?"

His fingers squeezed mine. "Franky, there are details I am not willing to share. I need you to breathe and listen to me."

In frustration, I rested my forehead on our joined hands and nodded. He kissed the top of my head. "My dad thinks I was spared the details, but I understand your brother paid the ultimate price." My head shot up, and my mouth snapped open. Crash nodded. "Your father tried to protect himself from—"

"From what? Is he in danger?"

"Not exactly. Uh ..." He fumbled for words. "Er, he hid some proof he'd acquired."

"Proof?"

His eyes closed as he continued his story. "Your dad challenged people my father is extremely cautious with." His eyes opened. "And that's saying a lot—not much rattles his cage."

"Crash, I know you're trying to explain, but you're confusing me."

"By the time the needles were forced into your brother's arm, we didn't know where he had been taken."

"Wait. Where was he? What do you mean we? Your family was looking for my brother?"

"Yes, but only... after my father kidnapped him."

My hands dropped from his. "What did you just say?" I sat completely stunned. I had willingly allowed the son of my brother's kidnapper into our home—in Tim's bedroom—in his clothing.

My ears rang from adrenaline as Crash rushed and rambled nervously through his next words. "Acting as if paranoid about *my* safety, my father said he had to cooperate with these men. He was forced to take Tim for some reason. That's how Tim and I became close. I was the one who brought him food and water. For enough money, people will turn against you, so my dad only trusted me to care for Tim, since he expected Tim to be returned home."

I thought that was a weird statement. *Does his father allow his minions to watch other kidnapped victims because they* won't *be returning home?*

"My dad was acting afraid of being in your father's position, with a stolen son. I believe I was also a target."

Still utterly confused with Crash's babble, my body sprung off the floor and slammed into his. Holding him to the ground, I growled like a lion. "Did you fucking hurt my Timothy?"

Crash didn't fight me. He lay there, allowing me to attack him. His only response was to say, "No. The opposite. He became my only friend, and I became his… That's how I know about you. Your father, unwisely, called the bluff of the ones threatening him—"

"What about the police?"

"None involved."

This made no sense. "My father didn't call them?"

His facial expression softened, showing sympathy. "No… your father never called them. He only spread false rumors about a drug addiction."

I shook my head in disbelief. "No. That can't be. He would do anything for us."

"Yeah? Then where is he?"

My growl returned. "He is working. For me."

"He has abandoned you the way he did your brother."

"You're a liar."

"I may be a number of things you will never approve of, but a liar is not one of them. Your father made a strategic move that would eventually help his future political career by gaining future sympathy votes."

"You're speaking as if my father was allowing my brother to die."

"Then you tell me what happened."

"I wasn't there."

"Maybe you should listen to what I have to say."

There was a moment of silence. "I want to hurt you."

"You'll want to do more than that by the time I'm through."

"Speak your venom."

"The media fell for the rumors and tips they received and wrote that your brother was in rehab. But the truth was—" Crash swallowed hard. "We were holding him ransom."

My jaw dropped.

"For a trade that your father adamantly refused."

The old newspaper article passed through my mind *"Todd Summers is sharing in the grief of losing a child... overwhelming drug problem in our town... 'I think it is time to take a stand... and fight.'"*

Why didn't he call the police? Why didn't he burn this city down to find Tim?

I felt a phantom knife slice my heart in two. I felt years of betrayal rake across, ripping my skin from my bones. Tim was gone. My only hope for a family member to love me was my father. And now I knew that possibility was a lie I told myself.

Crash wasn't lying, though. My father was not who I had hoped—dreamed—prayed he was. He would never help me with my mom because he had abandoned me.

Again, I found myself beyond weak as reality rocked my fake world. I collapsed on top of Crash's chest and whispered, "I hate you."

"I hate me too," he whispered back.

My anger toward my father was not Crash's. I was wrong to lash out at him. After a long moment of silence, I said, "I don't really hate you."

Crash's hand softly caressed my back. "I know."

"Crash?"

"Yeah?"

I sniffled. "Was he sad? Cold? Lonely?"

My body rose as he inhaled deeply. "Tim was never cold nor did he ever go hungry. He was locked in a basement bedroom of our lake house, but it is a guest room. Your brother's conditions were well above decent. He never even tried to escape."

I raised my head to look at him. "What? Why?"

Wrapping his arms around me as if to protect me from a possible past,

Crash choked out, "Because... they would have come for you." His hands grasped my face. "And now I understand why Tim willingly sacrificed himself for you."

My lungs filled with emotional cement. "No. No. No."

Crash held on to me as I tried to fight the loss of air. "They would come after you next, Franky. My dad believed your father would eventually surrender whatever info was being demanded. My father warned yours that these people are ruthless—"

"Who? Please tell me who are these people are, Crash. Please."

After a lengthy hesitation, Crash told me. "A Russian mafia of sorts."

I sat up on Crash's thighs, saying, "Wh-what? Wh-Why? My father was a CEO of—Jesus. Now he's running for office—what did he get into? What did he get Tim into?"

Crash sat up, forcefully holding me in his lap, saying nothing.

"I thought you weren't a liar." I struggled to get free.

"I'm not lying. I'm just not saying anything." He refused to release me.

"Let. Me. Go."

With one hand, he pulled the back of my neck, bringing my face to his. We were so close I could feel his breath. "Wouldn't you hold back information if you knew it would keep someone you care deeply for safe?"

My struggle ended.

I wanted to kiss him.

I don't know why, but Crash's words made me think of Link. I would've allowed him to think or demand anything of me and still kept information from him if it would've kept him safe. I nodded in surrender and motioned for Crash to continue to talk about what he could—or was allowed to—without bringing me harm.

Crash nodded. "But as the weeks went on, my father softened and became fond of Tim. Not my father's normal character, but Tim was so easy to like." He stopped talking, as if remembering qualities I knew my brother had. "So my dad tried *again* to convince yours he was playing with dogs that bite. We were shocked when your father finally conceded but thankful. My dad went to meet up with yours to retrieve a document. I was left behind with Tim. My dad had no indication that the mob was on to his fondness for Tim and would soon use it against him.

"The mob must have had the lake house bugged, saw a weakness brewing, and decided they needed insurance. As soon as my father left me alone, men came in, tied me up, and took... took..." Crash's eyes closed, as if going back to that night—back to awful memories that were making me ill, even though I hadn't heard them all yet. "Tim screamed for them to hear his plea, but they took him."

"But why?"

Crash stared at me but stayed silent. He wasn't going to share.

I blew out air and nodded. My safety was coming first again.

"I told them to take me, but they ignored me. All I can say, Franky, is there was more going on, and I wasn't a part of it."

I found myself wrapping shaking arms around my brother's kidnapper. I'm not sure if it was to comfort him or myself. I pictured Timothy calling out for help... with no one coming to his aid. And I was picturing a helpless thirteen-year-old boy being forced to witness it all.

Crash held on to me as if I were the first person to ever hear this horrific story, as if he had never been able to tell details and had been holding in all his pain. His voice shook. "They must have already known the document my father went to retrieve had been falsified—or guessed your father wouldn't come through. He didn't, but my father didn't know that. When he returned, he frantically untied and ungagged me, calling someone associated with the mob and pleading for them to return Timothy. On my father's phone, they showed Tim tied, lying on his side with needles being held to his vein as their final threat."

I loosened my hold so I could see into Crash's eyes, so I could watch him as he told me the incomprehensible fate of my only brother. "My father screamed into his phone, 'What do you want me to do to save his life? I have what you want!' That thick Russian accent echoed." Crash tried to mimic it. "Just want to remind you of what we do to traitors. How we will teach lesson. My father replied he had already learned that lesson well."

I wondered what that meant but sensed not to ask.

Crash took another deep breath. "Once they told him where to go for delivery, my father hid me in the old attic. As he went down the attic ladder, he said to himself, 'I will never show affection for the ones I care for. No one will know my weakness and use it against me ever again.' He raced away in his car to deliver the document."

"What document?"

Dead stare. Not sharing.

After a moment, Crash leaned his forehead to my shoulder. "What I *can* say is that the mob knew the document was not what they wanted because there were supposed to be two. Your father also knew this, Franky. Before my dad even returned for me, I heard screams."

His arms tightened around my waist. I knew the end was coming and let my tears fall onto Crash.

"I dared to look out the window of the attic and saw dark shadows on the boat dock. When the shadows got on a boat and left, only one shadow remained. I knew it was him, lying tied on his side," Crash whispered. "Tim was right outside the *whole* time, and we *never* knew it. Maybe… maybe had we known, we could have saved him."

I laid my head on his shoulder in unbelievable exhaustion, closing my eyes, trying to shut out the horrifying visions in my head—my brother alone, in the dark…

Crash began to cry. "Shit! He was still *alive* when I got to him… he was extremely groggy, repeating over and over '*watch over little T.*' Then… he died in my arms."

My head leaned back, tilting my distorted face to the ceiling as I moaned in complete inner agony. The one I had worshipped, as if he wore a shield like a true warrior, had died being my true hero. Heroes *do* exist. He wouldn't let the Russians come for me. I suddenly didn't feel worthy and wished I had been kidnapped instead. I wasn't as good—as selfless as my brother. I felt it should have been me who had died that night.

Crash grabbed my face again. "I'm so sorry. Maybe if I hadn't hid—maybe if I'd tried harder to escape when tied up—oh, God! I could've saved him! You could still have your brother!"

Me *still* having a brother was somehow resonating with Crash, as if he understood my anguish, but I was in too much pain of my own to ask how. I pulled him to me in a desperate, crying embrace. "Like you said, Crash. This is something bigger than the both of us. We were both too young to have any choices or any chances of changing the outcome. This is our parents' fault, not ours."

He shook in my arms as he broke. "I tried to do right by Tim. I tried to find you. But I was too young. He had never told me who your father was and *couldn't* so drugged at the end. Holding Tim, I pleaded, but he passed…

My father wouldn't tell me anything, out of fear for *my* life, he said. I had no idea you were so close to me. I assumed you were far—and all I knew was Summers. Tim had slipped up one day and told me." Crash squeezed tighter, "Do you know how many Summers there are in the United States?"

It was all making sense to me now. I pulled back to see him, so he knew I was telling the truth. As I wiped tears that refused to end, I said, "I was sent away. I stayed with my aunt for months… You weren't meant to find me, Crash. When I finally I came home… Tim was just… gone."

My parents had *led* me to believe my brother was simply a drug-head and had overdosed. I had always hoped they were wrong, and I'd been right to do so.

"But it should have dawned on me as your father became prominent in the community. Maybe I'd shoved the memory so deep that I refused to see what was in front of me the whole time." Crash seemed to punish himself with every word.

The next morning, lying next to me in bed, Crash looked through a couple of my medical books. *First Aid for the USMLE Step 1* and *Robin's Pathology Textbook*. "Are these the most boring books in the world?"

I chuckled. "Not for those who desire medical school."

He closed the books and set them back on my nightstand. "I'm not hearing desire in your voice."

"That's because it is not there."

"Then why read them?"

"I forgot. You've never met my mother."

My home phone rang.

Crash asked, "Speak of the devil?"

I had turned off my cell phone, and I'd refused to answer my home phone when my mom called. I just let it ring. The thought of hearing her treacherous voice made me want to vomit. I wanted to believe she had no knowledge of what happened to her son, but how could she not have? Wouldn't she at least have tried to visit him in the supposed rehab? That meant she was just as guilty for Tim's death as my father was.

"Don't want to talk with her this morning?"

The way he acknowledged my recurring morning calls let me know how much he was familiar with my schedule. I pulled our blanket higher. "How long have you been watching me?"

Silence and a stare were his reply.

So I answered. "They are both dead to me."

"I don't think you should let them know that you know the truth."

My home phone rang again. I was truly surprised by her effort to reach me. I closed my eyes, pulling the blanket over my head. "How can I ever look at them again? At least your dad sounded concerned for my brother. I can't believe I'm saying this, but it may be possible your father, a leader of a drug organization, is better then mine."

He pulled the blanket back down to see my face. "He didn't save your brother."

"But he tried. That's more than I can say for my father."

Crash rolled to his back and stared at the ceiling with his bare chest exposed. "My dad forces me to sell drugs because I can reach the young market. Addicting them to a drug that will forever be a monkey on their back ruins young lives. College scholarships down the drain… Dreams destroyed… Hearts broken… Lives lost so he can make mad cash."

"My father surrendered his son's life for his career." My stomach turned.

"I guess that makes us two of a kind."

I rolled to him. "Do you think… because they're our parents that… we're bad too?"

Facing me again, Crash answered. "I used to." He touched my face. "Before I met you. But you are proof that bad parents, bad people, can produce beautiful-hearted perfection."

My eyes closed. I still did not feel worthy of his affections. "What happens now? I feel we're trapped."

"*You're* not. I saw how you dance. That's your ticket out of here. You hear me?"

My eyes opened. "What about you?"

Still touching my face, Crash said with defeat, "I'm a lifer, baby."

My finger ran over the scar on his bottom lip, confirming his past owned him, and that terrified me. "Don't say that," I told him, shaking. "Don't say that." I attempted to touch the scar above his eye.

This time, he grabbed my wrist with some strength, restraining me. "Why?"

My jaw tightened before my body pushed against his, climbing on top of him. "Because I want to reach back in time and hurt whoever hurt you."

He froze, staring into my eyes.

I let him study me before slowly reaching my lips to that emotionally sensitive scar. Crash didn't move. He was finally letting me in. I didn't need to hear the story of how that permanent mark happened, I just wanted to somehow make my own mark on him—another way for him to remember the trauma—a trail of kisses. It felt so wonderful to shield him with my own body from any further harm.

His arms pulled me to him as he kissed me back with fresh passion. "I've never had someone care so much for me."

I kept kissing him all over. "I will always care for you."

When I'd learned Crash was my enemy, fate showed that to be a lie of the deepest kind. Trying to heal his wounds was helping me heal my own.

Crash was in the shower while I scrambled eggs, thinking about whether or not we could run from the truth. The loud banging on my front door and the constant ringing of my doorbell startled me into dropping my spatula. At my front door, I looked out the window and saw a black car in the driveway but saw no one but a driver. I turned to see Link frantically running around the outside of my house, trying to open the locked French doors. I realized the car must have brought him from the airport.

When he saw me rushing to him, he stopped trying to pry open a sliding door. Through the glass, he said, "You didn't answer your phones."

I realized it was Link who had been so constant all morning. I should've known my mom wouldn't have cared enough to put forth such effort. Link's forehead leaned against the glass in some sort of exhaustion and he began… crying.

In all the years I'd known him, I'd never seen him look so distraught. I ran to the slider and opened it in a hurry. "What? Link! What's wrong? Your aunt?"

He grabbed me as if relieved to see and *feel* me alive, kissing my head over and over. I inhaled every kiss. My body reacted to his warmth and comfort. My best friend was home, and it felt wonderful to have his familiar essence around me again. Everything I'd learned the night before had me on edge, and his embrace suddenly stopped me from falling. Yes, that was my Link, keeping me from falling apart again. Crash was right. Reether was my strongest link, not my weakest.

He kept repeating through heavy breathing, "You're okay. You're okay."

Even though my eyes were closed and I didn't want to let him go, my heart raced. Something was terribly wrong. "Link, please talk to me."

He gasped for air. "It's… it's Connie… She's… she's dead."

"*What*?" I screamed in horror. "When? What happened?"

He squeezed me harder. "A car accident."

Tears fell from my eyes. "Link, but why do you seem so worried for *me*?"

He went still before kissing my head again. "I'm just upset and wanted to see you—"

"Franky!" Crash's voice echoed through the house, cutting off Link. He ran down my stairs with a towel wrapped around his waist, his body dripping with water. "Franky! What's wrong?"

Link went rigor mortis stiff. "Son of a bitch," he growled.

Crash stopped when he saw Link. Crying about Constance, I put my hand on Link's chest to stop him when he took a step toward Crash. "Reether!"

Crash went pale. "Link, what happened?"

Link talked to him over my head. "Constance. Last night. Hit and run. No witnesses." Crash fell back onto the stairs, looking at the ground as if he was going to be sick.

Sobbing, I hugged Link again. "I'm so sorry. What can I do to help you through this?"

His only reply was, "Whit, move." He stared at Crash as if he was about to lose control.

I blocked his body with mine. "Why are you looking at Crash like that?"

Crash looked up at Link with such sorrow in his eyes. Link looked away then eventually down to me. "Because it just dawned on me that you slept with him. My girlfriend is dead, and you just had sex with the one who killed your brother."

I stood there with my arms around his waist, too flabbergasted to release him. My insides—that had been rejoicing in his touch—were now trying to communicate with my stunned brain. One part of me was trying to comprehend why Link would care who I had sex with; the other part was wondering why *I* cared that *he*… cared.

Crash cared too. He got up, trying to explain. “Link, that didn’t happen—”

Link’s chest bumped into me as he stepped forward, screaming, “Yes it did! Connie is fucking dead!”

I burst into even more tears. “Reether! I’m so sorry you’re hurting for her, but what Crash and I may have done has nothing to do with her death. If I could just tell you what I learned last night—”

“Whitney, don’t,” Crash interrupted.

Crash calling me by my real name for the very first time spoke volumes of the importance of what he was trying to tell me. *“Wouldn’t you hold back information if you knew it would keep someone you care deeply for safe?”*

I was at a crossroads. Tell the truth and put my very best friend in life-threatening danger with the Russian Mafia, or allow him to hate me? My decision was simple. It wasn’t a fight, just a slow surrender. I loved Link and always would cherish him, no matter what he would say when this particular conversation was over.

My arms slowly slid from Link, knowing what I had to do: protect him. Even though it was a lie, I suspected the importance of it to Link. I spoke words that would change everything. “Yes, you are correct. I slept with Crash.” Then I whispered, “And will continue to do so.”

Link, the young man I was sacrificing our friendship for, looked to me as if I’d stung him as deeply as possible. Then he stung me back with the very words I had said to Crash. “You make me sick.” Link turned away from me. Without looking back, he said in disgust, “Don’t come to her funeral.”

I stood with tears rolling down my face as he walked away from me. Link got into the waiting car without a glance back. Crash came up behind me and rested his hands on my shoulders. “You’re the most unselfish person I know.”

I had only one thing to say to my friend as I watched the black car back out of my driveway. “I love you, Link.”

I meant every syllable.

CHAPTER EIGHT

Tombstones and Terror

GROWING UP WITHOUT TIMOTHY TAUGHT me about loneliness. Living without my lifelong best friend taught me I wasn't as strong as I thought, that my persona was simply an act, backed by a blinking light in the night. Staring out my bedroom window, knowing Link was refusing to communicate with me, was when the void Link had occupied truly emptied. And instead of taking the time to heal that void—on my own—I ran to the next willing victim.

All my friends had turned their backs on me. The only contact had been from Harlan. It was in the form of a simple, yet highly appreciated, text.

He's in a bad way but made it thru funeral. I kno u'd want to kno. Give him time, girl.

At school, I felt like they were treating me as if I were sleeping with the devil for the simple joy of it. They all had known about my brother's death and acted as if the loss of him was more devastating to them than it was for me. No one took one moment to wonder why I would be with Crash. Crash being the only one willing to come near me was how he became my everything.

In his Lotus, I sat staring out the passenger window while Crash drove me to an unknown destination. "Where's my girl gone?"

I internally grinned, happy someone dared to still claim me, but I sassed anyway. "I'm not your girl."

Crash grinned. "There she is."

Inhaling deeply, I replied to his original inquiry. "I don't know where I am. I feel… lost thinking of Connie."

"You miss him."

It wasn't a question. Crash seemed acutely aware of what Link meant to me and how I was being affected by the loss of the deepest relationship in my life. "I'm sorry," was all I could say as a reply.

"For what?"

I chuckled in bewilderment. "I don't know. I guess for talking to you about another guy."

Crash went quiet for a moment. "It feels wrong to do so?"

My faced winced as I realized how this all sounded. "Ugh, yes, but it's not like that with Link and me."

"So I've been told," Crash quietly uttered.

"What'd you say?"

He half smiled. "I said, 'you look like you're cold,'" and reached over, closing my AC air vents.

"Oh, thank you." I wondered what he'd meant and why he lied about it.

We pulled into a parking lot, and I read the big sign. "Go-karts? Really?" I looked at him accusingly.

He smirked as he opened his door. "What? Your driving skills suck?" He shut his door before I could respond. That fired me up. *How dare he accuse me of poor capabilities and then deny me the chance to stand up for myself?*

I opened the passenger door, giving Crash—and any unfortunate patron within hearing distance, which happened to be the whole parking lot—a piece of my mind. "Who do you think you are to doubt my driving skills? I happen to be an excellent driver, for your in-for-mation, young man."

Crash walked to me, grinning. He softly said, "There she is again."

I pouted. "What does *that* mean?"

"I love that Franky spark inside you."

I'd been had. Crash had stirred me up on purpose. Deep down, I was thankful for the reminder of the fight in me. But of course, I could not tell him so and help inflate his hopeless ego. I headed to the front door. "This Franky spark is about to light up your ass. It's on! And gloves are off."

Heavy biker boots hit the pavement as he ran to catch up to me. "Did you say you are turned on while taking your clothes off?"

"*What?*" I shouted at him for changing my words around for his benefit. "Clothes off? You know, you're not right in the head." I kept walking defiantly.

He leaned down to my ear. "That makes two of us. Bring it, little girl—that is, *if* you can."

"Crash is about to crash and *burn!*"

He laughed as he held the door of the front lobby open for me. "I love it when you talk about getting me all hot."

"*What?*" I asked in dismay of his wordplay as I went to the register to buy our tickets.

Crash came to my side. "Put your wallet away." He pulled out his own.

I shook my head. "No, then you will expect another type of payment."

As he pulled out cash for the young lady waiting for our purchase, he growled, "You know I will. Tonight, as a matter of fact."

"But Mom said you have to stop touching me like that."

Crash froze, as did the young lady behind the counter, who also gasped. Crash looked at me with cash hanging from his shocked fingers that were attached to his shocked body. "*What?*"

"You remember, don't you?" I continued my obscene charade to win the battle of the Franky Spark. "Mom told us when she caught us in bed together last night that it's not the way a brother and sister should act."

And I walked away to find popcorn. *One point for Whit.*

The appalled young lady covered her mouth in disgust. Behind me, I could hear Crash saying, "No. She's just playing around. We're not *really* brother and sister."

He caught up with me at the concession stand, grumbling. "What game are you playing with me? See if Crash can go to jail tonight?"

"Oh, are we playing with handcuffs again? Like we just did in your backseat?"

As Crash's jaw fell to the concession stand counter, I casually told the flabbergasted young man who was waiting for my order, "People don't think Lotuses have a backseat, but some do." I looked at Crash to drive home my point. "As a matter of fact, it's a tight squeeze, but what does it matter when your boyfriend insists on you being in his lap?" I winked to send the message home. "Know what I'm saying?" Then I got back to business. "I'll have a large popcorn with *extra* butter please. I worked up quite an appetite." I winked to seal the embarrassing deal.

Somewhere in my *spiel*, Crash—unfortunately for me—caught his footing. Next thing I knew, his hand was in the air, waiting for the employee to give him a high five, yelling, "Holler if you hear me."

The guy looked stupefied, but slowly raised his hand and high-fived Crash while watching me, possibly picturing me in the backseat of a Lotus in Crash's lap.

As if I wasn't learning my lesson with the current status of the event, Crash said to the innocent young man, "Oh, your hand may be dirty now," and nonchalantly pulled cash from his wallet. He leaned down and mumbled to me, "We done?"

Totally frustrated and lost for what to do next, I went back to old tactics. I spoke to the young man who was now washing his believed-to-be dirty hand. "Sir, when you're done washing my tragic date off your hand, can I please add a large Coke, a hot dog, M&M's and a Reese's Pieces to my order? Oh, and that extra large bag of cotton candy hanging behind ya."

Crash happily pulled out more cash. "Good idea, baby. You'll need that sugar rush to keep up with your man tonight! I plan on a round two."

At that moment, I learned there were *two* young men who could handle Whit. I should've been celebrating the fact, but it saddened me to think that one of the two didn't want her anymore. Crash must've seen my expression because he leaned to me. "You okay? I was just teasing." He looked to the now confused employee and quickly explained, "We haven't even had sex. I was just joking."

I leaned into Crash's chest. His arms went around me. "You're not mad at me?"

My head shook no, and I wouldn't let him go. "Thank you." I was irrevocably full of gratitude for the friendship I'd found in Crash.

During our long embrace, my revenge order made it to the glass counter top. Still holding Crash around the waist, I looked at the abundance of junk food. "Sorry to have wasted your money."

A kiss landed on the top of my head. "Nothing, and I mean nothing, is a waste when it comes to you."

Crash and I formed a bond. Somehow, being with him made Link ignoring me more tolerable. It almost felt as if a piece of Link was still loving me. I needed that sensation. I didn't know how much until that sensation had been ripped away from me.

Another kiss landed on top of my head before Crash teased me.

"Besides..." He slipped the small package of M&M's in his pocket. "I can use these to coerce you into my backseat for real this time."

I laughed, hugging him tighter. Both actions felt good.

Crash continued to sell drugs while I continued to be exiled at school. We were from opposite worlds yet became joined in a reality that only the two of us were to experience. Crash became the only one I could turn to, the only one I could trust, so I clung to him... and fell in love.

"I'm not sure if you would want me here," I told the tombstone marking Constance's gravesite. "But I think Crash may be right. Missing you is also me missing Link. I'm mourning the loss of *two* friends."

To have Constance's banter and ridicule would have felt familiar—almost homey. It would've meant Link was around.

Her tombstone read:

Constance Ann Lordes

Beloved daughter, sister, and friend

I whispered in tears and embarrassment, "I was a bad friend to you. I am sorry." Shame had me looking away from the cold stone. I noticed matted grass to the right of her tombstone. In a spot of dirt, I saw a circle with water lines a finger had drawn—engraved into the earth. I wiped my unwanted tears and weakly asked, "Is this Link's spot, Constance?"

Feeling mortified to be jealous of a dead girl, I said, "I have no right to ask more of you, but... could I sit there?"

It's odd to be at a gravesite waiting for a reply, but I did, just like I always did at Timothy's bedroom door.

My legs took me to the matted grass, and I sat down, hoping to feel Link's remaining essence, hoping the seat would still be warm. It wasn't, but knowing he was clearly there often gave me comfort.

"You're probably wondering why I am here." I sniffled. "See, I have my senior project coming up. I'm tired for so many reasons and not sure if I can pull it off, and... Link doesn't want to talk to me. Maybe you could help give me courage the way Link would?"

Silence...

Feeling insane, I chuckled. "Or maybe not." After another moment, I told Constance Ann Lordes the truth. "You deserve his regular visits. You won, dear beautiful Constance. You won him in the end."

Even with all that was circling me like emotional, hungry vultures, my audition had been a success. One afternoon, when I entered the dance classroom, Mrs. P. excitedly grabbed my arm and pulled me to her office. She shut the door behind her and handed me an envelope. The hands Link claimed to be elegant shook as my fingers reached out to open and read my future.

On behalf of Tender West Dance Company, we would be honored if Miss Whitney Summers would accept our invitation to join our summer program…

I couldn't read on because the following words blurred with my joyful tears. Mrs. P. pulled me into an embrace, congratulating me for something we both had worked so hard for, and I sobbed with her—much needed—sincere affections. It would have been beautiful to share this moment with a mother who cared, or my best friend who I felt was a part of this life-changing moment.

My dance teacher rocked my body as she shed her own tears. "I'm not supposed to say anything, but…hints have been shared that you may also receive an invitation for permanent residency with their professional company at the end of the summer."

My shoulders shook as those words caused many emotions to rivet through me. My parents had warned me not get too attached to my "pipe dream," it being a waste of time, and to not get accustomed to living beneath my true potential. My future had been planned. A doctor I would be. But now my true potential was making my heart beam light rays that could be seen for miles. For the first time, I was to live a dream that I had earned on my very own. Instead of being terrified of my parents' ridicule, I was the most proud of myself I had ever been. I was to finish my senior year of high school and use dance as my ticket to escape from hell, just as Crash had told me to.

My loneliness for Link began to mold into anger. I started to feel that him abandoning me for sleeping with the enemy was wrong. Besides, it was none of his damn business and *definitely* not worthy of his disregard. I decided two could play that game, and I forced myself to not think of him. It didn't work, but I continued to lie to myself and say it did.

After another grueling rehearsal for my final project, the parking lot was empty. I expected some cars, since I had been released thirty minutes early, but I was alone except for the trees circling most of the property. My dance instructors said I'd worked harder than the rest, and being the only dancer left at the end of every school day proved that fact. I was so focused on how to tell Crash about my good news—and how to convince him to move with me—that I didn't jump out of the way until the last second when a car raced across the empty parking lot. Therefore, my foot was still exposed as the car rushed past me.

The engine roaring was loud enough so that I didn't have to hear the bones break in my foot, but not loud enough to shut out the pain. I never got a look at car because I was blinded with instant pain. It raced away as I screamed in agony, clutching my mangled foot.

Since he was all I'd had for weeks, reaching out to Crash was the first thought that crossed my scrambled mind. I'm not sure *what* I screamed to him when he answered his cell, but soon, I dropped my phone to the concrete I was lying on and tried to bear the worst pain of my life. It felt as if my foot had been run over by a lawn mower and shredded to pieces.

I woke in his arms as I was laid in the backseat of the infamous black car. He yelled instructions to the driver, but I couldn't make out the words. The pain was simply too overpowering. I had never been seriously injured, never broken a bone. I'd been completely unaware of true physical pain.

I woke again in Crash's arms as he rushed me through the emergency room's automatic sliding doors, screaming words that I could not register. As I looked over his shoulder, I saw the trail of blood my shattered foot left behind. Every droplet was a blood tear representing the end of my dream of dancing and escaping my building nightmare.

Crash laid me on a stretcher as curtains were being pulled around us. Only because of the medical books my mother forced me to read did I have an inclination of what was transpiring around me. A penlight was shined in my eyes, and common medical questions were asked as routine medical procedures took place. It was an out-of-body experience to be somewhat familiar with the medicinal lingo and strategies from a patient's perspective.

It was another reminder of the future I didn't want. An IV was inserted, and every drip was a haunting reminder of the unescapable future.

After my expedient X-ray, Crash kissed me over and over again until they forced him to stay behind as I was wheeled into surgery. Even in agony, I wondered why Crash had marks all over his face as if he'd been in a fight.

The bright room was cold, and so was I.

Soon the bright surgical lights faded… so did I.

I woke in a recovery room with strangers asking me questions. Then I woke again in a hospital room with different strangers talking to me. I was too sedated to remember the name of a button attached to a cord that was placed in my hand. I was told to hit that button when I felt pain.

When my eyes could finally focus again, I looked down to see what used to be a strong, blistered, dancer foot, now wrapped in bandage. The strangers were explaining how screws had to be attached to my bones until they healed… That the screws would be removed in three to five months.

I hit the pain button immediately for more than one pain. The view of my damaged foot reminded me that all my years of hard work were for nothing. All my determination to rebel against the administration of my God-awful parents had been a lost cause that I could not recognize until the pins and bandages represented the truth. I was to never be free of their control.

Crash was holding my hand when my eyes opened again. He looked terrible but tried to smile at me. "Hi."

"Do they know who hit me?"

"No." He shakily kissed my forehead. "We were hoping you could tell us something."

Officers came and asked me many questions I had no answers for and eventually left.

When my parents rushed into my hospital room and to my side, my mother actually looked worried, concerned like a mother of high quality and morals should be. Crash quietly watched from where he stood by my window with squinted eyebrows. Shockingly, I suddenly hoped Crash had been wrong and that my parents weren't the devil's spawn.

"Oh, my dear. I am here now," she cooed. My mom caressed my face with such affection. My heart easily opened and swooned, but she was only momentarily disguising her true being. I knew this because a flash went off, then my father showed my mom his phone. "Is this photo what you were looking for? You look extremely worried."

Her troubled face was for a photo op. Only another façade. Only another dream that had faded away like my foot's blood trail, only this time, the blood trail was from my heart.

I couldn't help thinking that, deep down, my mother was relieved my passion had been crushed and removed from the battlefield. She had ultimately won the war, and she knew it. Her inner celebration could be heard through words that cut deeper than the surgery I had just endured. "Don't worry… You still have Harvard. Dancing was only temporary; we knew this."

When my father saw Crash, his eyes showed instant recognition, even though he quickly tried to cover it. "Who are you?"

I couldn't help it. I vomited all over myself. It was all too much. Everything Crash had told me was now undeniably confirmed. My father was a creation of the devil. After the nurses cleaned me up, I lay there, crying, and I pushed the pain button yet again.

As if I had dared fate to make my situation even more volatile, Link charged into my hospital room to tackle Crash. Link yelled, "You were supposed to stay—"

BOOM!

I knew what Link didn't get the chance to finish saying. Crash was supposed to stay *away from me.*

Maybe it was because of my condition, or maybe Crash was simply fed up with everyone judging us and controlling our lives, but as my drugs took effect, he fought back, and the two young men became vicious. My mother's screams and my father's attempts to separate the bulldogs destroying my hospital room were the last things I heard before I passed out. I later learned that security came in and cleared my room of everyone, and nurses tended to my soiled hospital gown. I wish they could've cleansed my broken soul.

CHAPTER NINE

"For the both of us"

I SUPPOSE I SHOULD HAVE FELT special that my mother had stayed home with me for two weeks after I was released from the hospital, but I couldn't wait for her to follow my father and take off in a plane, leaving me alone again. Even her voice was too much of a reminder of her lies.

Security had banned Link and Crash from the hospital. My father had banned Crash from our house. I had banned Link from my life.

My cast had been temporarily removed to examine my incision. X-rays said I was progressing nicely. The screws holding bones together were doing their job. Now on crutches with another cast, I said goodbye to my mother as her driver carried her Louis Vuitton luggage to her car.

"I would love to stay, darling, but your father needs me. You understand, yes, dear?"

I faked a smile and played the game. "Yes, Mother, of course. I will be fine." I lightly sneered, "Have father call—if he can find the time."

"Of course, dear."

As her car pulled out of our long driveway, I lay on the couch, willing him to come to me. I closed my eyes and prayed for him to not abandon me the way everyone else had. I begged the universe to not make me endure loosing another Link.

I felt the cushion on my couch sink under Crash's weight. He whispered, "I love you."

Link had been right. It might not have been true 'adult' love, but it sure as hell felt like it. So I let myself *feel*...

Without opening my eyes, I cried out, "I love you too."

I had missed him so terribly that I was terrified to open my eyes and see that my mind was playing tricks on me. His hand touched my face, and I leaned into his palm so quickly you would have thought it was life or death. But I had to inhale his masculine scent.

"Shh," Crash whispered before his lips touched mine. Behind my closed eyes, it might have been dark, but in his embrace, there was light showing me the way to salvation.

We lay together on the beige leather couch in silence, just looking at each other. There was so much to comprehend—so much to digest. Timothy's murder, my parents, Constance, dancing, Link…

With a broken, fragmented heart, I finally said, "I will never dance again."

The words spoke of the simple movements on a dance floor but meant so much more. I was trying to describe the devastation I felt with the loss of freedom and the failure of being my own young woman.

He kissed my tears. "We'll find a way."

"How?"

Crash got up from the couch, and I instantly missed his comfort. He went to the stereo and found an old CD of my parents'. The song "Don't Stop Dancing" by Creed began to play.

This young man with a heart of gold put his arms under my body to cradle me close. As the melody with deep, meaningful lyrics speaking of so much more than dancing sounded through my living room, Crash began to dance—*we* began to dance. He smiled, trying to soothe my soul. "See, my Franky? You are dancing."

Dancing was the metaphor to not give up on life. I understood his message and was so touched by his efforts I found myself smiling at the guy holding me, singing *terribly* about believing I can fly… away.

"In yet another dark moment of my life, you have me smiling, Crash."

His blue eyes smiled. "Does this mean you're my girl now?"

A little pinch singed my heart as my head lay on his shoulder. "Yes, Crash. I'm your girl."

He kissed my head as he kept dancing and singing.

A memory I will keep with me always.

Whatever happened that day took Crash and me to another level. We let each other inside our souls, emotionally and physically. Our hearts and bodies connected. For a few days, Crash and I hunkered down in my home. I shared parts of me that had never been seen by another, and I loved every moment of his touches, kisses. I loved every moment of him, Crash, the one who showed me that through all the darkness, there is light.

I had been mentally and physically drained, but Crash gave me hope. I never knew how valuable something as simple as hope could be when you were on your knees feeling beaten and bruised. Crash's nickname, once again, suited him well, except this time it wasn't a drug I needed—just him. His presence and encouragement to not give up were my survival.

For three days, I felt safe and protected in strong, familiar arms. The only interruptions were my housekeeper or my tutor with schoolwork so I wouldn't fall behind. Other than that, I actually believed the outside world could no longer reach or affect us, but after a text Crash would not share, I knew the world had found us again and wasn't offering good news. Crash quickly became distracted and wouldn't divulge information about the cause of his mood change. I finished my school work, and my tutor left. On my crutches, I hobbled to Crash with a sense of urgency riveting through me. "What is it?"

He tried to smile and kissed my cheek. "It's nothing. Let's go."

Crash and I were on the way out my front door for a routine check-up for my foot when we saw Link waiting for us. Crash immediately took a protective stance in front of me, as if ready to pounce. "If you make me fight you in front of her and she gets hurt, I will kill you. Do you understand?"

I didn't say anything.

Link looked at Crash and nodded. "I understand."

Crash looked ready for more arguing before Link's words sunk in. He stopped. "Link? Is the cool Link back, or is the asshole in hiding?" Crash spoke as if he knew Link better than he should have from the few encounters they'd shared.

Link looked at the ground, as if ashamed. "Her mom thinks *I'm* the one taking her to the doctor today."

"Don't talk about me like I'm not here."

Crash moved from in front of me. Link looked at me. "I didn't mean for it to seem that way—just thought you weren't speaking to me."

I looked away. "I'm not."

"Kind of sounds like you are." Link's tone had me looking at his smirk.

"What's changed?" Crash asked Link in dismay.

After inhaling deeply, Link answered, "It dawned on me that I've known her"—he looked at me, as if to be sure not to leave me out of the conversation again—"you, I've known *you* all my life. And I know how much you loved your brother." The same could've been said about him. Link's recent actions and reactions didn't add up to how much he loved me. It would've—should've taken more than me having sex with Crash for Link to abandon me.

"Why the change of heart?" I wanted to confirm my suspicions.

He chuckled. "Can a man apologize in peace?"

Link's stubbornness had me shrugging, showing my own. "Fine. Anything else?"

"Well, I've been thinking. What are you two not telling me?"

Crash looked away with exposed guilt. I looked down, not able to lie to Link's face again. I became ashamed about the first lie.

Link watched us then nodded. "I see." He knew Crash and I weren't saying more on the matter. "Thought maybe I could go with you guys today?"

Crash looked at me in question. I was still angry at Link, but he wasn't the only one to blame, so I shrugged again. "I guess that's fine with me. If you're cool with it, Crash."

"I… I actually think it is a great idea." He stared at Link and warned, "Don't fail her again."

Link shook his head. "Never again." He sounded so sincere my heart opened up and welcomed Link back into my life without another thought. It was as natural as breathing.

After one look into Crash's backseat—not meant for adults of normal size—Link said, "I didn't think Lotuses had backseats." He smirked at Crash. "Now I see I'm right." I was confused why Link teased Crash as if they had been friends for some time.

But before I got to question the banter, it continued.

"It's a Lotus Evora, smart-ass, and that's considered a backseat."

"Whit, let's take your car. Where are your keys?" Link asked.

"Dear Mother took them, not convinced I would behave and not try driving myself."

"I'll go get my car then."

"No need." I chuckled, pointing to the tiny backseat. "And since your long legs aren't going to make it, Link—here, hold my crutches." I maneuvered into the vehicle.

Link looked worried, handing Crash my crutches as I stretched out my short legs across the little seat, but Crash just folded my crutches. "She's a bit stubborn and gets around unbelievably well without putting weight on that foot." He stuck my crutches in his trunk.

Link mumbled, "I'm well aware of her stubborn streak, Crash," while getting in the passenger seat. Looking back at me, he asked, "Are you sure you're okay back there?"

"Stop worrying. I'm a big girl."

"One: Big girls can't fit back there, baby."

"Two: Zip it, Link."

The ride to the doctor's office was long and quiet.

One: My mother insisted I go to the best doctor, so we had to travel to a bigger city.

Two: Everyone was in deep thought, and staying silent upset my stomach when I remembered Crash was hiding something from me. I was also nervous Link was going to push for answers I couldn't give. Keeping him safe was a priority.

In the multilevel parking lot, Link's and Crash's voices echoed as they both tried to help me out of the backseat—at the same time. Two sets of shoulders bounced for space.

"I have her, Crash—"

"I'm the one who has been caring for her."

Link stood abruptly, his bigger shoulders taking Crash with him.

"Whoa, whoa." I scooted toward the open passenger door they struggled at as if I was in any condition to stop a fight.

They stood face to face as Link said between his teeth, "That. Is. Not. Fair. Ninja."

There was a moment of silence as they stared at one another with heated glares. But suddenly, Crash's tense body softened, and he said under his breath, "I need her." This caused an unexpected change in Link's body language, and he stepped away, clearing the path for Crash. As Crash scooped me out of the backseat, I watched them, completely baffled. My voice shook. "What is going on? Why did you call Crash Ninja, Link?"

Two sets of eyes stared at me, admitting to nothing other than their plans to not tell me anything. *Damn it.* Link retrieved my crouches, and the conversation was over.

In the doctor's office, I sat on the examining table as the doctor explained positive results from my X-ray. Link stood a little behind me. As I was told I was healing nicely, Crash kept aggressively texting on his phone, but when the doctor tried to confirm what I already knew, that my career was never to be, Crash put his phone in his front pocket. "So when does physical therapy begin?"

Link shakily plopped into a chair beside me, looking pale as a ghost. I don't think he'd understood how severe my injury was and how crucial his friendship could have been during such a heartbreaking time for me until that very moment. And no one knew better than him how much dancing meant to me.

The doctor nodded, understanding Crash's interruption. Crash had already told me he didn't want me to hear my crippling fate over and over. He wanted me focused on the future getting brighter. The doctor explained my turning points and when to expect what, but I was too distracted by the unnerving outcome. Freedom. Gone.

I looked up from the cold, bleached-looking floor to see Link staring at me with raw emotions lurking in his eyes—ready to burst through his last shred of control. I simply and sadly nodded. My fate and path were irrevocably paved into hell. I guess it had been from the beginning of my time. I just hadn't known it yet.

Once we were all back in the car, I sat in the backseat watching Crash who was again aggressively texting as if completely frustrated. When he stopped, the three of us sat quietly inhaling and exhaling through the stress that seemed to mount even further. Our internal questions—no one dared speak out loud—could almost be heard. We kept looking to one another as if... *bonding*, knowing we needed each other to survive whatever was to come next. We didn't know what it was, but it was coming nevertheless.

As the Lotus purred down the road, Link broke the silence. "I'm so sorry, Whit."

I sat in the backseat blowing out air, trying to keep from crying. I was exhausted and wanted to stop shedding tears over every heart-crushing blow. Crash reached back and took hold of my hand, but instead of feeling reassured as normal, I sensed his unease. "Link... I need you to love her."

Meeting his eyes, Link sounded choked up. "I do. I *swear* I do."

They stared at each other. Crash only moved his eyes to occasionally see the road. They were communicating, but I was being left out of the silent conversation yet again. I wanted to scream, *"Tell me!"* but being a stubborn fool myself, I easily recognized true stubbornness. So I tried a gentler approach. "Please talk to me, guys." I was not to be answered.

Finally, Crash nodded to Link as if understanding more unspoken words, gripping his steering wheel so tightly his knuckles went white. He struggled to swallow as he pulled into my driveway. I kept watching his nerves rise, making me struggle to swallow as well. Crash put his car in park, shut down the engine, but he never took his keys out of the ignition. That meant only one thing to me—he wasn't staying.

It felt like the center of the earth trembled, threatening to open wide and consume me whole. I wanted to stop time and not hear or feel what was coming next, but Crash spoke his next shocking words to Link, and I almost died. "I need you to love her, then, enough… for the both of us."

My mouth opened, but I'm not sure I was inhaling as I watched Crash pop his trunk then exit his car. Dumbstruck, Link got out and folded his seat forward for me. Crash walked to Link. "I mean it. No questions. Just man up and take care of her."

Link's body tensed. "W… what do you think you are doing?"

I was becoming so alarmed I felt my ears burning. Next thing I knew, Crash was gently lifting me from his backseat and cradling me in his arms as he had the night we'd danced in my living room. The tears I'd tried to hold back for Link fell uncontrollably for Crash. Link watched us as if he understood exactly what was happening. I didn't. I was clinging to Crash's neck, crying. "Why do I feel like this is a goodbye?"

Crash rocked me as if he treasured me the way my brother had. Then with regret, he said, "Because it is." Crash looked at Link. "Get her stuff from my car." Crash being older never felt evident as it did in those moments. Link nodded in disbelief but did what he was told, putting my crutches by my front door.

I wailed in horror. "No! No! You can't do this to me!"

"I have to, Franky."

"Why?" Even with all the evil that was in our lives, I couldn't think of one reason good enough to force us apart. We had bonded! We'd made love!

We were together—*we* were what made me want to continue to fight even though I'd lost so much!

Just then, the black car that represented where Crash came from pulled up in my driveway, telling me this was really happening, and they were here to make sure of it. I screamed, feeling as if my insides were being macerated beyond recognition. Crash held me to him in a desperation that could have touched the coldest of hearts and whispered in my ear, "Whitney."

My name. He used my name again.

I went quiet.

Crash kissed me and continued. "My father says I am a danger to you, that the mob has learned we are together… and… *they* are the ones who hit you."

"W… why?"

"You know I can't say. I must keep you safe. That's all that matters."

I was tired of not being told what was going on. I was tired of not having a say in my life. Mentally melting in despair, I cried out, "I don't care if I'm safe! I don't care if I get hit daily. Just don't leave me."

Watching us, Link sounded gutted. "Crash. Don't do this to her—"

"I have to. Don't make this harder on me, Link."

I rambled in desperation. "Don't go. I'll endure anything for you. Please, Crash. Please."

Crash looked at me with an expression saying he believed me but refused to allow my self-sacrifice. Forehead to forehead, he whispered, "Oh, my God. This is the hardest thing I have ever had to do."

"Then don't do it." I grabbed his face, his shoulders, anything to keep him from leaving what we had built, together.

He pulled me to him, holding me tight, inhaling me. Then he stopped and pulled back. With tears of his own forming, Crash told Link, "Take her from me. I can't—I can't let her go."

Link didn't take me. "Crash, I—fuck! There must be another way—"

"TAKE HER!" Crash screamed, as if dying. "FUCKING TAKE HER FROM ME!"

I wailed in his agony and my own. "PLEASE DON'T DO THIS!"

"TAKE HER!"

Link seemed to recognize the plea and reacted as if on instinct. As much and as hard as I fought it, Link took me from Crash and cradled me in his arms. "Shh, I'll figure something out." While Link tried to console my hysterics, Crash's shaky hands held my face. He kissed me, and I knew it was our last.

"Please. Please," I tiredly sobbed.

Crash grabbed the back of Link's neck and looked him in the eye. "Keep your promise."

Dumbfounded, Link nodded with wide, scared eyes.

One of Crash's guards approached. "It's time." Crash's eyes met mine again as the big man pulled Crash toward the black car, and I had never seen eyes so tortured.

Another of Crash's father's employees got into his Lotus and drove it away. While Crash was being shoved into the black car that had taken me to the hospital and was now taking Crash away from me, he yelled, "I love you! I love you so goddamn much I'm willing to let you go! Do you understand how much that is? Franky! Tell me you know how deep our love goes!"

Clinging to Link's neck, I nodded through unspeakable tears because I had never felt so loved in my entire life as I did at that very moment. Crash nodded, as if relieved I heard him, his meaning, his truth.

Crash's door slammed shut while he continued to watch me as if he'd never see me again. And then, because of circumstances completely out of our control, Crash was driven away… from me.

CHAPTER TEN

Choice and Chance

NONE OF MY CALLS OR texts went through. Crash's number had been changed. After not hearing from him for weeks, one would think I would've begun to heal, but I didn't. I all but gave up.

My eighteenth birthday came and went. I hoped to shrivel up and die, but I wasn't so lucky. Link kept his promise to Crash and kept me alive, made me go to school, made me live another day. He practically moved in with me, insisting on staying with me every night until one evening we had a… disagreement, and I asked him to leave. It may have seemed foolish, but the argument was monumental. And I was not of sane enough mind to differentiate the problem from the solution because Crash consumed my every thought.

I hadn't moved in hours. I never even bothered to change out of my white, gown pajamas. The day passed, and the night arrived. I just sat on the beige couch, feeling such despair that I could hear the silence of my world. My ears could literally detect molecules in the air as they buzzed around me. Or maybe I was simply losing my mind.

Since no one from school ever called anymore, I had already talked to my mom for the evening, and Crash had stopped calling all together, when my cell phone rang, I answered without looking. "Link, I just need the night to think. Stop worrying."

"Maybe it is not Link who should be worried."

I froze.

The deep Russian-accented voice sounded more sinister than anyone I had ever heard. "Ah. Already worried?"

My voice sounded as dry as my mouth. "Yes, I am worried."

"Good," he said as I sat in the dark. "I love to have someone's undivided attention."

I closed my eyes and tried to breathe to stay composed because my instincts were screaming that I was in huge trouble, and so was Crash. "You have it, sir."

"No wonder little Crash likes you so. You are a smart little cookie." The way he spoke of Crash and as 'little' confirmed how he viewed us as inconvenient chewed gum on the bottom of his probably expensive shoe. "Do you know what it is that I am looking for?"

"No. No, I do not."

The phone went dead.

I stood up, staring at my phone. That was the only communication I'd had with someone who could hurt someone I loved, and I'd just screwed it up! Right before panic set in, my phone rang again, and this time it was through FaceTime. I answered, seeing a stranger smiling at me over the video chat. The light from the phone glowed against my face. He had dark hair, spooky blue eyes, and a gruesome scar above his upper lip. He looked like he might once have been handsome like Crash, but like Crash, he carried scars that told a story of a challenging upbringing.

"Forgive my rudeness. I just thought this way would be more persuasive for you."

He was much younger than I had expected, and I couldn't fathom how someone so young could be already so calculating and cruel.

Just then, the automatic timer turned on lamps in the house. I jumped. With my heart pounding like a jackhammer, I nodded. "Again, you have my full attention."

The phone's view moved. "You hear that, Crash? We have her full attention."

I could barely make Crash out because it was so dark wherever he was, lying on his side with his hands tied in front of him. He looked as if he was trying to say something, but his lips were too swollen to move properly, and so was the eye I could see. As my knees buckled and I unwillingly sat back down, I reached my shaking fingers to my phone, somehow hoping to touch him, heal him, knowing that they had ruthlessly beat him, but I stopped when I saw what Crash's weak finger was pointing at.

Link's carved water sign on my very own dock.

The man showed me his own damaged face again. "Crash is… oh, how do I put this? Uh, indisposed at the moment."

I knew where they were, but I played the game my mom and I had played most of my life. I gulped down fear and horror and tried to sound as cooperative and sincere as possible. "Sir, I will do whatever you ask of me. Anything. Absolutely anything, just give me a chance before you hurt him anymore."

He grinned. "If only your father had been so easy to work with."

My eyes closed again, and I begged myself not to think of my brother and lose my shit. I needed to stay focused and prevent Crash from dying. When my eyes reopened, I said, "I wish the same. If he had, my brother would be alive. Because of this, I hate my father beyond words and do not care what happens to him in order to keep you happy and Crash alive and well."

"I do think I believe you." He sounded a bit astonished.

"My actions will prove you are right to do so. What do you want or need, and where can I find it?"

He rolled his eyes. "This is where our troubles begin. I cannot tell you what I want—or I have to kill you both."

I nodded at my impossible task. "A dilemma I'm willing to work around, seeing how I wish to live."

He laughed to someone nearby him. "I really do like this American girl."

Hearing this guy liked Whit charm, I decided to apply it a little thicker, gain any points or seconds I could to help Crash and myself through this horrid mess. "Would you believe I have a thing for Russian men?"

"You don't say?" He purred through his Russian accent.

"It is true. If we had the time, I would show you where I wrote it in my diary under 'foreigners to conquer.'"

Proudly, the Russian said, "You are impressively quick on your feet, especially at such a dire time."

I looked down to my cast. "Not as quick on my feet as I used to be."

"Now that I know how charming you are, I certainly would like to go back in time and rectify my error."

Finding my old groove, I said, "Well, thank you, Russ. Do you mind? I have a thing for nicknames."

"And your charm continues. I now feel we are bonding, for me to have acquired a nickname from my American friend."

"Maybe someday we can laugh over all this with a cup of tea—wait, I bet vodka is more your speed, huh, *Russ*?"

"Vodka is from the gods. Tea is from shit."

I tried to laugh, but it came out as a fake, nervous choke. Trying to recover, I said, "So, can you at least tell me what the thing you're looking for looks like? Do you know if it is here?"

"Again, I do not wish to kill you."

"Again, we agree R.U.S.S. Tell me, what's rambling around in that magnificent brain of yours? You must have a plan. Don't all mob leaders *lead* because they have great plans?"

He chuckled. "I am not head of our organization. This work is beneath *him*." I heard a touch of judgment similar to the one I had with my mom. That was when I suspected I was possibly dealing with the head honcho's son. "But the answer to your question is yes, there is a plan, though you may not like it."

"Well, you're clearly *leading* this mission, and I'm not liking my boyfriend looking a bit mistreated there behind you, so try me. I'm open to suggestions."

"I wish to send one of my men inside your home."

"Oh," I said with a whole new fear. "Now I see why you assumed I wouldn't be too excited. Can you at least promise your man doesn't have a young-girl fetish?"

"When I like someone, I tend to become violent if this person is mistreated. The men I'm in charge of do not like putting me in this state of mind. It causes bodily damage to them and their loved ones."

"Now don't I just feel all warm and fuzzy inside. Hey, Russ, if I say yes, can I come outside and see him?"

Russ went quiet, then finally said, "I slipped up, eh?"

"Don't beat yourself up about it. I'm just a good listener, and there were *signs* everywhere."

"I do believe you *are* a little treasure." The word 'treasure' rolled off his Russian tongue, as if he found it pleasurable. My eyes welled. I was speaking with someone who was present when my brother had begged. Russ replied to my original inquiry. "My insurance shall stay separate from you."

I tried to smile and stop my tears. I shrugged, as if unaffected. "Can't blame me for trying, right?" Then I said with an uncertain confidence, "I'm turning off my alarm and will meet your man at my back sliding door." I was confident I was doing the right thing to help Crash but uncertain of how I would endure.

Hours... It took hours of searching—hours of me hoping Crash was breathing out there on my dock, so close yet so far from me. My home looked vandalized by the time they'd succeeded. Russ had sent in three more men to search. The sun was rising when one of the men said something in Russian from upstairs. When he came down, he was slipping two pieces of paper in his jacket. They looked like certificates or something, but I couldn't understand the writing because the one I could see wasn't in English. He left with the other three men.

I waited at my back sliders with my cell phone in hand. I had been up all night and was exhausted. I had been instructed not to leave my home, so I didn't. I just watched most of the men load into a black SUV that was now crudely parked in my backyard. Standing at a back open passenger door, Russ got on his phone while looking at me through the glass. "Hello?"

It was unsettling to watch him talk to me through his phone. "I wanted to thank you personally for your honesty and cooperation."

His tone was different. I nervously said, "You're welcome. May I come outside now?"

He nodded, so I opened the doors and slowly hobbled on my crutches across my back porch, but I stopped when he said, "But it saddens me to not return the favor."

My breath caught. "I don't understand. I did all that you asked."

"Yes, but Crash's father did not. A debt is a debt." Russ got into his transportation and closed the door as some sort of signal. A man leaned over Crash, and as the syringe emptied into his vein, I knew exactly how Crash felt to watch the same happen to my brother. Utterly hopeless.

The night Crash and I met raced through my mind... his smile, his eyes... *him*. I thought of how we—how Crash and I were meant to be. I hadn't known at the time how much was still to come, how much had been and was being done in the shadows of my past and future by those who loved me. And by those who didn't.

Crash was calling out to me. The drugs were taking affect. "*Franky*!"

I screamed. I screamed and took off running toward him, not caring about my injuries or cast. My thumb frantically searched for the buttons for 9-1-1 as I tried to hold on to my crutch. I knew it was against the rules to involve the authorities, but what else could the Russians do to hurt me? They'd killed my brother, my dream, and now were killing Crash. But my hand simply could not manage both tasks. By the time I was to my stairs at the edge of my decking, I lost hold of my cell. Trying to catch it had me abandoning one crutch, causing a tumble down the stairs, losing both. Everything slowed as I saw the phone land mid-fall and then take the crushing blow of the crutch and my weight, breaking my only means of getting Crash help.

I was on my own.

Not having a clue of what to do once by his side didn't stop me from rolling to my knees and attempting to rise. My casted foot had landed at an awkward angle, promising agony, but I still pulled myself off the ground, saying the hell to the future damage to my older injury, and limped as fast as I could toward Crash. Pain shot through my foot like lightning bolts.

As I ran with a pathetic hobble, the man with the syringe did the unthinkable. He rolled Crash into the water. I knew Crash was too drugged to swim, to stay afloat. Not caring about the repercussions, I wailed in horror as Crash disappeared from my sight. As I crossed my ridiculously sized backyard, the remaining man got into the SUV, and they raced away, leaving deep ruts in my lawn. The lawn now looked like my life—full of deep scars.

Temporarily, any pain felt from my injury disappeared as my focus went solely to Crash. I was to the end of my dock in seconds, leaping into the water, cast and all, not thinking of how the fiberglass would soon fill and become a weight.

The rising sun gave me just enough light to find him sinking. Instead of swimming up for air and trying to save my own life, I kicked to go deeper into the blue waters. His eyes were closing. Crash was dying right in front of me.

Not being able to reach his lifeless hands, I frantically grabbed on to the front of his shirt. My fist, Crash's only lifeline, held tight. I began the unbelievable struggle to get us both back to the surface. My want, my need to save the young man trailing beneath me wasn't enough for the impossible task. With every kick of my foot, incomprehensible pain claimed my nerve endings, overwhelming me. My need for air compounded because my heart was hammering hard, dealing with intense adrenaline. My cast and injury had become the grim reaper announcing my undeniable death. I thought of my brother's words about me having no buoyancy as Crash and I continued to sink.

The water swooshed and bubbled with my struggles, my fight, but soon it became a choice—a choice to either let Crash go and save myself or to never let go and follow him to the end. I thought of the ballerina and her shoe... her metaphor. I looked at Crash and suddenly understood her passion, her reasoning, and her effortless sacrifice, because to live without Crash was too devastating to conceive.

Silence followed as I stilled and allowed destiny to take over.

There was a beauty in dying that day, one I did not expect when I had imagined meeting my maker. The blue waters we sank through were angelic, quiet... peaceful. I thought of Timothy again and how he had once told me he would always be in these waters, waiting for me. Maybe he was right...

Link glided through the crystal waters as if he belonged to the gods of lakes and rivers. He forced himself to plummet deeper into the blue waters that were drowning me, drowning Crash.

A lake was killing me that day. No, I take that back; my *decisions* were killing me that day, and he knew what decision had been made. As Link swam toward me, even faster, his expression was one of horror. He knew what decision I had made.

The sun shone, lighting his way to me, to Crash. Link's youthful blue eyes were so determined to reach me, so determined not to let me go, so determined to see me fail in my attempt to give all...

I'll never forget the touch of his skin as his fingers stretched up from beneath me, touching the tips of mine. It was a sensation only recognized by one passing, saying goodbye, giving up, surrendering to the life I no longer wanted to live. I looked down to see Crash touching me, telling me he was still alive and not to give up. That was all I needed to change my mind and try to live. My hand let go of his shirt, and I grasped his palm tightly, telling him how much I loved him.

With my other hand, I reached up to the one rushing to save us—Link, my friend. My outstretched hand told him how much I needed him and for him to swim as if my life depended on it—because it did.

I found a beauty in dying that day…

I found a beauty in living, too.

India R Adams

Empowering Perfect Imperfections

Thank you *so* much for reading *Blue Waters,* A Tainted Water Novella. I hope you enjoyed it! Whitney, Crash, and Link's story owns a piece of my heart. If you would like to read more of their journey in the second Tainted Water Novella, *Black Waters,* for FREE, please leave a review for *Blue Waters* at any online retailer of your choice. Then tell me you did so by following this link http://indias.productions/contact. *Black Waters* will be yours to download!

ABOUT THE AUTHOR

India R Adams is an author/singer/songwriter who has written YA and NA novels such as *Blue Waters* (A Tainted Water Novella), *My Wolf and Me*, *Steal Me* (A Haunted Roads Novel), *Rain* (A Stranger in the Woods Novel), *Serenity* (The Forever Series Novel) and also The Forever Series music.

India was born and raised in Florida but has also been so lucky as to live in Idaho (where she froze but fell in love with the small town life), Austin, Texas (where she started her first book, *Serenity*, and met wonderful artists), and now Murphy, North Carolina (where the mountains have stolen a piece of her heart).

Being a survivor of abuse has inspired India to let others know they have nothing to be ashamed of. She put her many years of professional theater background to the test and has written fictional stories with a shadow of her personal experiences. She says, "I'm simply finding ways to empower perfect imperfections."

Another cause India feels needs change is sexual slavery. She has joined forces with jewelers to design beautiful ways to raise money for nonprofit organizations. Even though India writes about serious subjects such as domestic violence, sexual abuse, and human trafficking, she has a magnificent sense of humor, as do the characters she creates. Perfectly balanced between laughter and tears, her readers see how to empower their *own* perfect imperfections.

CONTACT THE AUTHOR

http://indias.productions

Twitter.com/TheIndiaRAdams

Facebook.com/IndiaRAdams

SPOTLIGHT ARTISTS

With every book I release, I am giving attention to up-and-coming artists that, in my opinion, are simply amazing. Drumroll, please! In celebration of my debut release, I want to give a very special shout-out to *two* separate artists. Two very talented young women whom I admire deeply. Mieka Pauley and Ashley, lead vocalist in Chasing Jonah. When I saw each of these artists perform live, I saw hardworking musicians with incredible drive and heard incredibly unique voices. Mieka Pauley and Chasing Jonah will both be spotlighted again in *Black Waters*. Mieka Pauley will also be spotlighted in *Destiny*, book two in The Forever Series. So stay tuned...

To find out about Mieka Pauley's or Chasing Jonah's tour schedules, or to buy their music (that is mentioned in *Blue Waters*), please visit their websites:

http://www.mieka.com
http://chasingjonah.com

Or visit iTunes or other digital music store outlets.

And yes, I am accepting nominations for other artists that my readers feel would be great with my work. Email me your submission at india@indias.productions

ORDER OF NOVELS TO BE RELEASED IN 2016 BY INDIA R ADAMS

Black Waters, second novella in **The Tainted Water Series**

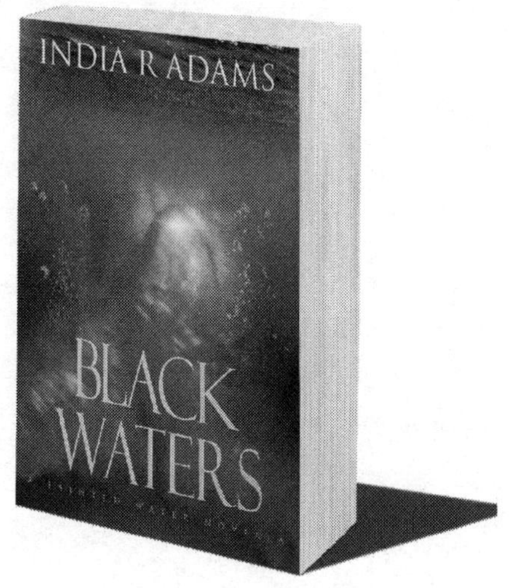

My Wolf and Me

Steal Me, book one in **The Haunted Roads Series**

Rain, book one in **A Stranger in the Woods Series**

Serenity, book one in **The Forever Series**

INDIA'S THANK-YOUS

There are so many out there that I want to thank for the past seven years but cannot have my thank-yous longer then this novella. So I will save personal gratitude for each book they were involved with.

As I have said, "It takes a village." So, thank you to my team at India's Productions. Without you, well, there would be no me.

Beta readers, you absolutely rock my world!

Thank you to my editors, Karen and Lauren, for helping my words come to life.

Thank you, Lynn (Red Adept Editing), for being so unbelievably patient with me, an author trying to find her way.

Travis, I LOVE my covers!

Jessica and Christi, you won't let me fall, and I love you for it.

To my mama, who passed before my first book release, but is my biggest fan in heaven.

To my daughter for drawing Link's water symbol.

And, a very special thank you to my family, especially the ones who had to live the everyday process of writing eighteen books: my husband and children. My life gave me a surprise in the healing process and that was becoming a storyteller. Even though it was more than challenging at times (and you had to cook dinner more than once, lol), look, we did it!

I love you, I love you, to infinity… Roger, Billy, Cheyenne and Dezeray, you are my world.

SONG LIST THAT INSPIRED INDIA FOR BLUE WATERS

"All the King's Horses" by Karmina
"Love Me Like You Do" by Ellie Goulding
"Heroes" by Alesso (featuring Tove Lo)
"Am I Wrong" by Nico and Vinz
"Trumpets" by Jason Derulo
"Superheroes" by Script

Made in the USA
San Bernardino, CA
27 November 2016